I0547995

# The Diary of an Innocent

Des Birch

This book is sold subject to the condition that it shall not, by way of trade
or otherwise, be lent, resold, hired out, or otherwise circulated without
the publisher's prior consent in any form of binding or cover, other than
that in which it is published and without a similar condition including this
condition being imposed on the subsequent publisher.

The moral right of Des Birch has been asserted.

First published in Great Britain by Pearl Press Limited

Copyright © 2010 Des Birch

All rights reserved.

ISBN:  0956651844

ISBN-13:  978-0956651846

*To Julie my Warrior Queen and to Sarah and Martin of whom I am very proud*

Des Birch

# CHAPTER 1

I have never thought of myself as a bad person. I still don't. I have led an ordinary life with my wife and our two children. I still lead that life. I am not a religious person, only attending church at christenings, weddings and funerals, although I was raised as a Catholic.

The difference now is that I understand where I fit into the whole scheme of things. I used to admire people who die for their faith, from the saints of old who were persecuted, to the latter-day martyrs who use explosives and die by their own hands, or by the hands of others.

I had drifted away from my religious upbringing and from its umbrella of safety, which I felt I no longer needed. Why then did I still feel pangs of guilt when I drove my family to church?

Had I been indoctrinated to the same extent that a long-term prisoner can become institutionalised? Was there another life outside religion, or was it simply I who was failing God's test?

I do not believe that a person simply abandons a long-held belief, without having something to replace it. It is still there lurking in the annals of his mind, ready to flood over him in times of crisis. And so I had drifted into this limbo, getting on with the rest of my life and letting those who had the calling, get on with that part of it.

These are people who have the strength of faith that I never had. Yet now I look upon them with sadness. I see them as misguided children: good children who obey their parents without question, without the slightest comprehension of what the rules mean or how to apply them.

My wife, Alison, saw the effect this was having on our relationship and I felt that I was betraying her by not sharing my thoughts. Yet, I had to rationalize the whole thing in my mind before I could share it with anyone, even her. Finally, she gave me an ultimatum, phrased in the tender words that only a loving wife uses. If it was important, then I should write it down and share it with the world; if not then I should forget it, and we could go back to leading a normal life.

I will never forget what I have learned and so I have pieced it together and written it the best way I can. I have drawn no conclusions, at least not on paper. I have left that task to people far more learned than I. I have simply attempted to record my interpretation of events as accurately as possible.

# CHAPTER 2

The day began like any other warm August morning in London. I was swept along by the crowds of commuters, down steps and escalators and onto the platform, finally squeezing myself into one of the silver tubes that streak around under the busy city streets. I stood there, bodies pressed against mine, people with lifeless eyes and blank expressions, trying to detach themselves from this unnatural place. As the train lurched and swayed in the semi-darkness, the strong body odour of the short man in front of me was beginning to make me feel ill. A couple of times I had scratched my nose, to give myself some momentary relief from the stench but eventually I had to turn my head. As I did so, I caught the eye of an attractive, well-dressed woman in her late thirties, whose expression of panic at this sudden contact brought a smile of friendship to my face. The icy glare that was returned cooled my smile and as my

4

cheeks relaxed, my head turned back and my eyes once again fell upon the underground map at which I had been staring. The stench had returned, but now I treated it as a penance. I had sinned, broken an unwritten rule. I had invaded her territory, her own private world. For this, I must atone. I did not look round again.

The doors opened and as we all spilled out onto the platform, even the thick oily smell that hung in the air seemed fresh. In the distance, along one of the tunnels that led to the freedom of the city streets, I saw a beggar sitting propped up against a wall. I approached him and felt in my pocket for the small amount of loose change I had left. His head turned in my direction, the last vestiges of what had once been hope, reflecting in his eyes. I dropped the loose change into his hat and his expression changed to one of sadness. It seemed to say 'is that all I'm worth?' I wanted to tell him it was all I had, but I remembered the woman on the train and I carried on walking.

A man in a suit passed in the opposite direction with some coins in his hand. I turned to see the beggar's reaction to his offering, but he was looking the other way. The man pocketed the coins and quickened his pace. Perhaps he understood the rules better than I did.

The slight breeze and the bright sunlight of the city streets soon eradicated the memories of my ordeal underground and a smile once again swept over my face. Today was going to be a good day. I would pick up my first wage packet for four months.

Could it have been only a couple of weeks ago on that dismal wet day when I was beginning to lose hope of ever finding another job, that my luck took a turn for the better?

I had looked out of my living room window when I heard the Mercedes cough, splutter and finally bounce its way to an undignified halt outside my front door.

The man got out and slammed the door, rain bouncing from his shiny head and forming patterns on his pale grey suit.

He stood there for a moment, stroking his grey beard in silent contemplation before deciding on a plan of action. As he walked to the front of the car, I wondered how this well dressed man would cope with the grime under the bonnet.

I did not need to be able to lip-read to understand the profanities that came from his mouth as he kicked the tyre, spraying water over the bottom of his trousers and splashing his shiny shoes.

I opened the front door and stepped out under the porch, mildly amused at the actions of this funny little man.

"Problems?" I asked rhetorically.

"Bloody thing won't start!"

"Come in out of the rain for a minute," I said to the man whose luck seemed to be as bad as mine.

"It's been back in the shop three times in as many months. The last time they assured me they'd sorted the problem! Bloody garages!"

I led the man into the kitchen and put on the kettle while he took off his jacket and shook it.

Alison came in at this point and finished off the tea as I sat down at the table and chatted to the man.

"It's not been my week," he continued. "I hired a labourer last week. He only came in for two days, didn't do a lot of work and I haven't seen him since. This is holding up the whole project. A site can't run without a labourer. Still, you don't want to sit here listening to my problems. Could I use your phone to call the auto club?"

I led the man into the living room to use the phone and then I returned to the kitchen.

"He needs a labourer," said Alison excitedly, as soon as I entered the room. "Why don't you ask him for a job?"

"I was thinking about it, but I don't want him to feel obliged, just because I let him use the phone."

"Why ever not? One good turn deserves another."

When people look at me they see a big strong man wielding a sledge hammer on a building site or sinking a pint with my mates, but I am really quite a shy person. I hate awkward situations and always avoid them whenever possible. To ask the man outright for a job based on the help I had given him was something I could not cope with. That is probably why Alison and I get on so well together, we complement each other's shortcomings. She is a small, petite woman who can cope with any situation; I am a hands-on rugby player who works hard and protects his family. It is the perfect relationship.

The man returned to the kitchen and thanked us for the tea and the use of the phone.

"So you're looking for a labourer then?"

Her forthright approach made me shrink back in my chair.

"Yes, I need one desperately!"

"Then look no further," she continued. "There's one sitting right there in front of you."

And so it was that the man was only too happy to offer me the job right then and there on an old house he was renovating in west London.

# CHAPTER 3

Everybody looked happy as I entered the huge old Victorian house and put on my work-boots.

It had once been a magnificent building with its three stories and huge bay windows. The gardens, now overgrown by years of neglect must have stretched to half an acre. Having good mental imagery, I could picture the house as it was in all its splendour. I could see women in big hats, roaming the immaculate gardens, handmaidens in attendance. I wondered about the secret liaisons held in the hidden arbours and behind the hedgerows of the garden, all conducted with the politeness and shy diplomacy of the Victorian gentry. I saw servants milling around the house creating ease and comfort wherever their masters or mistresses would go. How amazing it would be to live in such a place as a Victorian gentleman.

My first job of the day was to clear out the rubble from two rooms that had been knocked into one. By the time we sat down to eat our sandwiches for morning break, I felt that I had done a good few hours work. I had a wall to demolish after that, which I was really looking forward to doing. Not that I have a destructive nature. Far from it, but every time I swing the sledge- hammer, I am thinking of Alison and the children, knowing that I am doing this to put food on the table. I swing the hammer harder. I am the hunter, working hard to secure their future. After all those weeks out of work, I finally felt like a man again.

The demolition of the wall was now complete and I wiped the sweat from my brow with my sleeve. I had worked hard and done well.

I loved this old house and felt a little sad at having to knock down a wall that had stood for many decades but it had become so unstable that the only possible course of action was to krock it down and rebuild it. I consoled myself with the thought that I was helping to restore the building, not destroy it.

I collected two scaffold boards from the driveway and carefully placed them between the door and the skip outside. This was where I would run my wheelbarrow to clear out the rubble this afternoon, but now it was time for lunch.

There was a buzz around the site, as the boss's car was outside, indicating that the wages were being given out.

"You've done a good job these last couple of weeks," he said as he handed me my wages. "Have a good weekend and I'll see you on next week."

It was not so much the praise that made me feel good, but the sense of being wanted. Another week of hard work, another pay packet made me feel I was back in the mainstream of life. A little comment that made me feel very proud.

After lunch, I continued my work with renewed vigour and had cleared most of the rubble from the room when I noticed an A4 size book poking out from beneath a lump of concrete on the floor. I picked it up, blowing the dust from the cover, and flicked through the first few pages. It seemed to be an appointment book. I looked inside the front cover and I could just make out the name Fr. Pat Ryan. A priest's appointment book! Wishing that it had been something more exciting, I tossed the book onto a pile of rubble and carried on working. I would finish clearing this room by the end of the day.

Whether the book did not want to be thrown away or I was having second thoughts about it, I do not know, but as I was shovelling the last bit of rubble, the book slid from my shovel and onto the floor. I picked it up and tossed it into the wheelbarrow.

There is something very satisfying about finishing a job. I had tipped my last load and my thoughts returned to Alison and the children. Maybe we would go out tonight to celebrate. I turned the wheelbarrow and saw the book lying on top of the pile, staring at me. I picked it up again and flicked through its pages again, some of which were stuck together. It had become damp and the writing was barely legible.

While the early part of the book was indeed nothing but appointments, the rest of the pages were full of writing. I thought that it might contain some of the history of the house we were renovating and that it would be interesting to learn something about it, before we changed it beyond all recognition. Being honest with myself however, the real reason I brought the book home was pure nosiness.

The Journey back through London could not dull my mood. I grinned at all the commuters, ignoring the looks of panic and the icy stares. I grinned at a pair of nuns on the platform who gave me the all-knowing 'God loves you' smile. I grinned at the station worker who gazed at me with hollow eyes. The biggest grin of all was for Alison as I showed her my wage-slip. The hunter had brought home the kill.

The evening went well. We took the children out for a meal and tired them out with constant chatter about the future and the exciting holidays we would have. The future for a six and an eight-year-old was what would happen the next weekend, so we included that as well.

I told Alison what the boss had said. The job was only a temporary contract, but I knew he had more work. Indeed, he had already asked me if I wanted to work on another site when this one was finished. Alison had often told me that she was proud of me, but that night I could see it in her eyes. We put the children to bed as soon as we got home and stood for a moment, watching them slip into timeless dreams of beaches and donkey rides. I put my arm around Alison and led her into the living room where we uncorked a bottle of wine.  I have never felt closer to my wife than I did that night as we made love in front of the fire.

# CHAPTER 4

It was Sunday evening before I opened the diary. Alison was in the bath and the children were tucked up in bed. I took a long, thin knife from the kitchen and carefully set about prising apart the pages that were stuck together. It was not a difficult task as there was only a block of about fifteen pages that was really damp, and this was only on the edges. The task completed, I opened the book at the beginning.

Much of the earlier part was written in pencil: Mrs. so and so re. Baptism; catechism class held half hour later today. I felt like a spy, reading a secret document behind enemy lines. Sometimes I found it difficult to decipher parts of the faded scrawl, but I stuck to the task and soon I was used to it and managed to read it at a reasonable pace. About a quarter of the way through the diary, the writing changed to fountain pen. This was smudged and far more difficult to decipher, but it was now beginning to get interesting. It started to give me an insight into the priest's life.

Alison had now finished her bath and I decided to leave the book until after work on the following day. However, this did not happen.

The week was filled with working all day and taking over the task of amusing the children in the evening. The school term had not started for Emma, our elder daughter, and the girls had worn out their mother all day, so it was only fair that I took over the responsibility for them in the evening. This was what I told Alison but, being truthful, I really looked forward to spending time with them. We had promised them a trip to the seaside on the Saturday and most evenings included vivid descriptions of the beach and the amusement arcades, of candyfloss and toffee apples. My excitement was genuine. I am sure we have children just so that we can play in the sand and eat fish and chips while paddling in the sea, without anybody thinking we are strange. I do pity people who do not have children. They must miss out on so much of life.

On Friday evening, as I was explaining to the children how sandcastles became real cities when everyone had left the beach, I noticed their mother watching from the kitchen doorway. She walked in with a big smile on her face, sat beside me and rubbed the back of my neck.

"It's time for bed now," I whispered to the children.

"But daddy," cried Emma. "You haven't finished the story yet!"

"Please tell us the ending," said her sister, Chloe.

I wavered a little as it was past their bedtime.

"Yes come on," said their mother. "We all want to know what happened!"

So did I! I had not thought that far ahead yet, but with all three of them ganging up on me, I had no choice and the children went to bed a little later than usual that night. I do love being a dad!

I put the children to bed as Alison made a cup of tea.

"You should write them down, you know," she said, as I sat down and she handed me the steaming cup.

"What?"

"The stories you tell the children. You used to like writing stories when you were at school."

"It wouldn't be the same," I replied. "I love to watch their faces at the exciting bits. I wouldn't get that if they just read a book."

"Well why not write them for all the people who don't make up stories for their children?"

"All parents tell their children stories."

I sometimes think that Alison has some strange notions about how other families interact.

We watched a couple of short programmes on the TV, before the ten o'clock film was due to start.

"We've got to get an early start tomorrow if we're going to miss the traffic," I said.

Alison stroked her hand across my chest and kissed me on the cheek.

"Then we'd better have an early night."

Suddenly the film lost its appeal as my hand hit the off button on the remote. This was one story I would not be telling the children!

# CHAPTER 5

Saturday morning came and we ushered two very sleepy little girls into the car and made our way to the coast. We missed the heavy traffic and all was going well until Emma woke up and asked me for the first of many times:

"Are we there yet?"

Alison smiled at me. We had been discussing how long it would take one of them to ask the question and which child it would be.

"Not long now, darling," she said as we passed the sign that read: 'seafront 8 miles'.

The day was very hot and the beach crowded. After stepping over bodies and walking around towels and parasols, we finally found a small patch of sand to call our own.

Our nearest neighbours were a group of three raucous nineteen-year-old lads, drinking can after can of cheap beer and whose language left much to be desired.

"Oy!" I called to them. "Watch the language, there are children about!"

The youths gave a cursory glance in my direction and carried on as before. I will not stand for bad language in front of my family so I took three easy strides towards them and kicked the can out of one of their hands. The youths jumped to their feet at this sudden confrontation. I grabbed one of them by the upper arm and threw him into his mates.

"If you want to get drunk and use that kind of language, go and do it somewhere else," I commanded.

The three looked at me for a moment, but saw in my eyes that I was not about to back down. They picked up their towels and their beer and grumpily exited the scene.

As I turned round, a couple lying kissing on the sand, flashed into view. I looked again and felt my blood boil as I realized that they were two men! I looked at the girls playing in the sand. They had not noticed them.

The men were too much wrapped-up in each other to notice my approach, so I moved one of them with the sole of my foot. He rolled off his mate and the two lay there staring at me. I spoke quietly so that the girls would not hear.

"If you two want to do that sort of thing, do it in your own homes."

"Who are you?" asked the one I had moved with my foot.

"I'm the one who's telling you to get out of here!" I said.

The man was about to reply but his mate wisely prevented him from speaking, saying that they were about to leave anyway. Immorality is the other thing from which I will always protect my girls.

Having sorted out the problems, I walked back to Alison and the girls, ready for whatever game they wanted to play, now that we had a little more space. The girls decided that they wanted to build sandcastles, so I took them to a nearby gift shop to buy buckets and spades and of course, flags for the sandcastles. These were chosen with extreme care as the little people who would take over the castles later, would have to know which ones belonged to them. Building sandcastles is a craft that I rediscovered a few years previously. It required the right amount of water mixed with the right amount of sand and the right story to go with the building project. If I had boys, the castles would probably have been at war with each other. The girl's stories however, were usually of princes and princesses, and their ensuing betrothal. Today was no exception and the castles were well under way, when Emma noticed something missing.

"Daddy," she said in panic. "Where are they going to get married? We have to build a church!"

"Mummy can build us one over there," I said as I nudged Alison's leg and pointed to a spot on the sand.

"Oh no she can't!" was Alison's instant reply.

I gave her a puzzled look.

"That's the main road past the castles. You can't build a church in the middle of the road! How would the horses get round it?"

I had not realized she had been following the plot!

"Yes, silly daddy," said Chloe. "You choose where it goes mummy."

"And I thought that I was supposed to be the master builder!"

Alison, as always had a reply.

"You be the builder and I'll be the planning office."

"Yes," said the girls in unison, although I am certain they did not have the least idea of what a planning office was.

The work was eventually completed. Mummy had a little trouble with the steeple but we all helped out and with a little more water, many hands and a hastily found excuse for not building it very high, it was just left to me to complete the story.

"What time do you think the little people will come tonight, daddy?" whispered Emma

"About seven o'clock." Alison's quick reply took me by surprise. I had opened my mouth to answer, but her sudden reply prevented me from closing it as I turned to look at her.

"Just about the time little girls go to bed?"

Of course, Silly daddy!

The girls slept all the way home and barely awoke as their mother undressed them and put them to bed. We were quite worn out too, but it had been a good day and it was not very long before we were tucked up in bed as well.

Sunday morning came and I drove Alison and the girls to church. Virtually the only times I used the car during the week were for shopping and church. It was easier to take the tube or the bus to work or for days out in London.

Alison often asked me why I did not come into the church with them but I would always use my get-out clause. I would ask her what she thought was wrong with me, that going to church would change. This of course was unfair but I did not know the real reason. I suppose that the nature of my work often obliged me to spend my Sundays knee-deep in building rubble. This, coupled with having got out of the habit and not being able to associate the events of two thousand years ago with my present life, persuaded me to abstain from these ancient ceremonies that were reproduced all over the world on a daily basis. It did not stop me from feeling guilty, however. The teachings of my childhood were still deeply rooted within me.

I went for a walk and sat in a nearby park where I opened the diary. Fr. Ryan had been making detailed notes about his daily work around the parish. This story was interspersed with his daily schedule of meetings and services.

# CHAPTER 6

Sat. 15<sup>th</sup>.

Spider, a fierce-looking nineteen-year-old with web tattoos covering his hands and arms, was leaning against the wall of the youth centre that Fr. Ryan helped to run. The priest had known Spider since he was a wild twelve-year-old. It was a common story among the youth of this area: A violent, drunken father combined with an inadequate mother. The only respect he could command was one of violence on the streets. If you were not a member of a gang, you were alone and vulnerable.

"Morning Spider."

Fr. Ryan always used their gang names as a mark of respect for their culture.

"Father."

He nodded as he addressed the priest, but there was a look of mistrust on his face. They were both in uniform: one wearing the badge of peace, the other the badge of war. They were the leaders of rival gangs and respect had to be shown on both sides. Every time they met, it was like a meeting of foreign diplomats from two warring nations.

"Are you coming into the centre today?"

A nervous smirk came over the youth's face, as he looked round to see if anyone else was watching him. Image was everything.

"What for?"

The priest was ready for this. Attracting a gang member into the centre was not an easy task. There was 'street-cred' to think about!

"I've got some furniture to shift and I need someone with a bit of muscle. I'm getting too old to be shifting it on my own. Fancy giving me a hand?"

He had been saving this job for such an occasion and was pleased with the way he had phrased the question. He had shown respect by using his gang name and by indicating that he was a fit, strong man. Spider also owed him for all the times he had defended him in his many conflicts with the police.

"I've got business to take care of."

The local youths always had business to take care of, yet they seemed to spend the daylight hours standing on street corners, looking menacing. Perhaps this was their business! The priest stretched out an arm in a guiding gesture.

"It won't take long."

The youth glanced around once more, as he made his way to the door.

Spider's attitude changed the moment he entered the youth centre. It was safe to relax his guard for a time, which almost never happened in his world. Mrs. Bryant, who ran the centre, looked up in surprise as the unlikely pair entered. She smiled, but traces of suspicion still showed. Gang members would usually look in the door solely to attract the attention of a younger sibling, to get him to run an illicit errand.

"Nice to see you back here, Eric."

Spider's body stiffened at the sound of his real name. She had known him in another time when he used the centre regularly. But he was not Eric the child anymore; he was Spider!

"Spider has kindly volunteered to help me clear out the back room," interjected the priest.

Mrs. Bryant, realizing her mistake, set to putting the record straight.

"Thank you, Spider. We were wondering how we were ever going to shift that lot. Do you think you can manage it between you?"

"We'll manage."

Spider was a man of few words, but there was a lot of hidden meaning in his actions. He flexed his muscles and the half-dozen sixteen-year-olds who were sitting at a nearby table, looked upon him in awe. Honour had been satisfied and the two leaders made their way to the storeroom.

There was indeed a lot of work to do. Old furniture and rubbish had been piling up in the storeroom for years. Perhaps the priest had understated the amount of work, but Spider had agreed to help and he could not back out now. They talked as they worked, but the priest was always careful not to speak badly about the youth's way of life. He had to show understanding and gain his trust. This was difficult as Spiders life was built around image and physical power. Neither side could show weakness, yet Spider saw in the priest another form of power. A power he did not understand, one built on attitudes he always considered to be weaknesses. The priest must be powerful to have the audacity to ask a gang member to move furniture, yet he posed no threat. He thought that this man must have no fear, speaking to members of opposing gangs as if they were all part of his congregation.

Nothing could be further from the truth. Fr. Ryan was all too conversant with the dangers of gangland life. He had watched helplessly as young boys and girls became entangled in its powerful web. People throwing away what little hope of a future they had, to enter the world of drugs and violence. A dangerous world in which many died young and even more suffered a life of crime, degradation and dependency

He wondered what the church could do to reach these people. What use is preaching from a pulpit if the people who need to hear you are not there? This was not what religion should be about. It should be about attracting more people into the church, not damning the people who do not come. He smiled to himself as he imagined the reaction of his congregation to two gangs taking their places on either side of the church at Sunday mass! This was a frivolous thought as it would never happen, but he allowed it to continue. Rival gangs trying to out-sing each other to the hymn: 'The Lord's My Shepherd!' What a coup that would be!

Fr. Ryan did not want to delve too deeply into Spider's private life, as this was the first real talk he had with him for a long time. It was better to chat about other matters. He did ask him not to smoke inside the centre, but without any reference to what he was smoking. Spider simply shrugged and stood at the back door until he had finished.

The work continued for an hour, when the priest went into the main hall to get them a Coke. It was a hot day and they both deserved it. A figure lurking in the entranceway caught his eye.

"What can I do for you, Donkey?"

The aptly named, massive bulk of a twenty-year-old youth wavered in the doorway.

"Seen Ron?" he asked in the usual stilted conversation of a gang member.

Ron was a fifteen-year-old youth who ran 'errands' for the gang. Donkey was a member of one of Spider's rival gangs and the priest saw an opportunity to talk to two opposing gang members at the same time.

"Come in for a minute," he said as he approached the youth.

"Can't," he replied. "Business to take care of."

"It won't take a minute," said the priest. "I need to shift a pool table and we haven't got the muscle in here to do it."

Power again. This was something they understood. The youth glanced around to see who was watching.

"All right, where is it?"

"Just over here," said the priest as he led the way across the room.

The pool table did not need to be moved. It would be moved occasionally if more room was needed for a meeting, but the priest saw it as a way to bring rival youths together in a common cause, however small.

"Come and grab the other end of this table," he called to Spider.

As Spider entered the room, the look of hatred between the youths was electric. They both glanced at the priest. Had he betrayed them by this simple act? This was no look of rivalry. It was much deeper. But they were on foreign soil; on his turf, and he would be the mediator.

The huge body of Donkey strode to the table, never taking his eyes off his adversary. As his podgy hands gripped it and lifted it to waist height, his belly spilt over the cushion. He stood there holding the table, without any hint of strain on his face, fixed stare slicing through the air. The slim figure of Spider, arm muscles bulging, lifted the other end. As the priest guided them across the room, the wordless conversation continued. The youths at the table had stopped talking and were watching the events unfold. They too understood this silent language. The table slowly sank to the floor and the silence was broken as Donkey pointed a finger in the direction of his rival.

"I'll see you later," he said threateningly.

The two stared at each other for another few seconds when Donkey abruptly turned and walked out. The slamming door broke the tension and the priest turned to Spider.

"How about that Coke now?"

"Got to go."

"Business to take care of?"

"It may not be important to you, but it is to us."

"It is important to me," said the priest.

"What's important to you? You know nothing about our business!"

"Then tell me!"

This was developing into an argument, which was exactly what the priest was trying to avoid. He put his hand on Spider's shoulder, feeling the tense muscle.

"Come and see me again. We can talk."

Spider shrugged off the hand and left the centre.

"Thanks for your help," the priest called after him, but there was no reply.

That could have gone better, he thought to himself. Had he handled it the right way? Had he in fact gained anything at all? At least they still had enough respect not to cause trouble when he was around. Not that he could have done anything physically to stop them if they had. These were powerful youths who lived their lives by fighting.

"It's a dangerous game you're playing there, father," said Mrs. Bryant. "Best to leave well alone."

"They're only kids," he replied with far more conviction than he felt.

I closed the diary at this point, as it was time to pick up Alison and the girls.

# CHAPTER 7

I arrived at the church just as the last of the congregation was leaving. I was usually sitting in the car by this time, to avoid talking to the priest. I expect I felt guilty at not going to church. Not that Fr. Dan said anything to make me feel this way. He was a modern priest; one you could talk to as a friend without being preached at. It was my own upbringing that made me feel guilty.

"Hello," he said, hand outstretched in greeting. "Nice to see you."

As we shook hands, a pang of guilt once more swept over me and I felt that I needed an excuse for not attending mass.

"Sorry I didn't make the service," I said as my mind raced to find an excuse. The priest, perhaps seeing the quandary I was in, came to my rescue. He first looked at Alison and then down at the children.

"You have a lovely family here. That's what Christianity is all about. The church is just here to help, and we will always be here for you."

This seemed to me to be a radical statement. What about the sacraments? What about attending mass on Sundays and holidays of obligation? In hindsight, the statement the priest made was an obvious one, but it did not make me feel any less guilty. I thanked him and drove Alison and the children home.

That afternoon was spent playing with the girls. It began with a game of Twister, but soon developed into an all-in wrestling match with Alison encouraging the girls to jump on this 'beast of a daddy.' I thought the game was unfair because every time I was winning, their mother joined in to even up the sides! I do not know where children get their energy! After tea, we settled the children in front of a video, and Alison washed the dishes as I dried.

"What was that book you had with you at the church?" she asked.

"Book?"

"Yes.  The one you were trying to hide from the priest!  Naughty, is it?

She smiled when she made her last comment.

"Don't let the girls see it, will you?"

"No, it's only a diary."

"You, writing a diary?"  She said in amazement.  "That'll be a first!"

"It's not my diary.  Just one I found on site."

"You're reading someone else's diary!  Whose?"

"A priest's."

"You're reading a priests diary!"

I was stabbed by a pang of guilt and felt that I had to explain about wanting to learn something of the history of the house I was working on, but Alison knew me better than that.  All I could think of saying was:

"There's nothing much in it."

Even though I had turned my head, I could feel my wife's muted laughter. I turned back and she could no longer suppress it. I smacked her on the bottom with the tea towel and we cuddled in a fit of childish giggling.

I returned to the diary that evening after the girls were tucked up and Alison had settled down to watch her regular Sunday-night programme.

# CHAPTER 8

Mon. 17<sup>th</sup>.

It was almost midnight and Fr. Ryan was on his way to bed, when there was a loud hammering on the door. He hesitated, thinking it was probably a drunk on his way home from a late-night session. The hammering continued. He walked to the door, making sure the chain was on before opening it.

The hunched-up figure of a youth was leaning against the doorpost, blood running from his mouth and nose. There was a gaping wound just below his swollen eye. The priest hurriedly unhooked the chain, glancing around the empty street as he ushered the youth inside.

"Sit down Spider. I'll get the first-aid kit."

The youth slumped down in the chair and the priest attempted to clean his wounds. Spider dismissed this offer and the priest felt a vice-like grip on his arm.

"You said you wanted to help," said the youth, still breathless from his exertions.

"I'm trying to help!"

"Then hide this for me."

Spider took a small handgun from his pocket and offered it to the priest. Fr. Ryan knelt there, staring at the weapon.

"I can't do that," he said quietly.

The look on Spider's face was a cross between anger and disappointment as he slipped the gun back into his pocket and tightened his grip on the priest's arm.

"If you don't want to help, then you've seen nothing. Understand? Nothing!"

The fire in his eyes as he used the priest's arm as a crutch to help him stand, told Fr. Ryan that the conversation was over. But the priest could not leave it at that. He had finally achieved his aim of having a gang member ask for his help. How could he now refuse him? The question of the gun worried him. Perhaps it would be safer to keep it off the streets. Because of the youth's weakened state, the priest managed to push him back into the chair.

"Wait," he said.

The youth's muscles tightened. He was not used to being challenged.

"Please!"

Spider relaxed a little as he waited for the priest to continue.

"Just tell me one thing. Has this gun been used to kill or injure anyone?"

The relevance of this question seemed to puzzle Spider but he once again removed it from his pocket and held it out for the priest to take.

"No father, we've never used it. I just can't be caught with it or I'll go down."

The priest took the gun. He had never handled a small firearm and was surprised at how heavy it was.

"Why do you need a gun?"

"Business."

"The business of killing people?"

"Protection," replied the youth.

Fr. Ryan knew that he would get no more information than this and indeed, it could be dangerous to try.

"All right," he said with a sigh. "I'll take charge of the gun if you let me clean up your cuts. They could become infected."

The youth thought for a moment before nodding his assent.

"Was this fight anything to do with what happened at the youth club on Saturday? Asked the priest. "I'd hate to think I'd caused it."

"He don't need a reason to cause trouble."

"Who doesn't? Donkey? Was it Donkey who did this to you?" Silence. "Oh I know. It's just business."

"Right."

The priest dressed Spider's wounds and the youth muttered a muted 'thanks' as he left. Coming from anybody else, this would have seemed ungracious, considering the magnitude of the deed he had performed, but from Spider, it was a rare honour. Fr. Ryan carefully wiped the gun with a cloth and tucked it away safely in a drawer, resolving to hand it into the police when he was out next.

Tue. 18th.

At ten-thirty pm, Fr. Ryan sat down to watch the late film. People are often surprised at the thought of a priest watching a film. They seem to think that a priest's life consists entirely of talking to God and conducting religious ceremonies. Priests have to relax sometimes and watching a good film was something Fr. Ryan really enjoyed. A loud banging was heard on the door. Remembering the events of the previous night, Fr. Ryan walked to the front door, wondering if he would be greeted by another broken body in need of repair. The three youths standing on his doorstep stank of hard drink and trouble. He wished he had used the chain but it was now too late.

"Hello father," said the tallest of the three. "Let's talk inside."

The priest was shepherded into the living room and pushed unceremoniously onto a chair. He did not recognise the youths but they wandered round the room with a confidence inspired by gang membership. The priest was frightened, but dared not show his fear. He went to stand up but an outstretched hand with palm facing him persuaded him to stay where he was.

"Nice place you've got here," said one of the youths, handling an ornament that he had taken from the writing desk. "Pity to see it wrecked."

The menace in his voice was evident and Fr. Ryan was even more frightened now. He did not even know to which gang they belonged.

"What can I do for you, lads?"

The youths ignored the question and the priest once again attempted to stand. This time he was prevented from doing so by a hand gripping his hair from behind. His head was held back and the youth's other hand was holding something against his face.

I hear you're looking after something for us, father. You'd better keep your mouth shut about it because you know what we do to people who can't keep their mouths shut, don't you?"

The priest did not, but he knew it would not be pleasant. He decided it was better not to reply. The fewer words he used to these people, the less chance he stood of inciting violence. He heard a click and a silver blade flashed in front of his eyes.

"We cut out their tongues!"

This last comment was whispered in his ear and the strong smell of whisky was almost choking him, yet he dare not move. As if a silent bell had been rung, the blade clicked back and the youths left the room.

"I know we can count on you, father."

The voice was almost pleasant and the front door slammed shut.

The priest sat there for some time until his body stopped shaking. What had he got himself into? He remembered the comment that Mrs. Bryant had made. Perhaps he was in over his head! He had imagined being able to get the gangs together, perhaps at the youth centre, and reason with them. Until this moment, he had still looked on them as youths who needed a bit of guidance. Now that he had begun to enter their dark world, he realised that they were no longer misguided children. These were fit, young men who lived a life of violence and were capable of killing each other, and maybe even him! This last thought made him shiver as he remembered the switchblade. His work put him in a vulnerable position. How could he have been so naïve? He turned off the film and prayed for a way out of this mess. His thoughts turned to Christ at Gethsemane and he wondered if God, in fact, had wanted him to continue with this, despite the outcome. He had often prayed for an inroad into the youth culture, but so that he could help and understand them, not hide their weapons and implicate himself in their crimes. Now that his prayers had been answered, his first thought was to run. He tried to rationalise what had happened. A youth he has known for years does a stupid thing by getting hold of a gun. He probably never had any intention of using it. He did not want to be caught with the weapon, so he gave it to someone he respected for disposal. Then a few of his drunken friends became frightened and protected themselves in the only way they knew how: by threats. The rationalisation made him feel better. Why then was he still frightened? He had done nothing wrong. He had hidden the gun as he was asked to do. He had not mentioned it to anyone, as he was threatened not to do. He had done nothing wrong. By whose rules? Was he now beginning to think like a gangster? Were his concepts of right and wrong now being dictated by the threat of violence?  No, he must not let this happen!  Why had he hidden the gun?  Because he was frightened?  No, he did not feel threatened at that time.  He took it merely as a token of good faith so that he could break into the culture he wanted to help. He had no intention of returning the gun, or of mentioning it to anyone else, so the later threats did not influence his actions in any way.  Still he was nervous.  What would happen if they asked for the weapon back?  He would tell them that he had handed it into the police anonymously.  Would they believe him?  Would they see this as an act of betrayal?  These were violent men who swiftly dealt with acts of betrayal.  He must act out of a sense of right and wrong rather than fear.  However, if they did see this as an act of betrayal, all the trust he had built up over the years would be lost.  His getting hurt would serve no useful purpose.  Perhaps he would hang on to the gun for a little longer.  It could not harm anybody where it was.

Sat. 22$^{nd}$.

The priest had got over his ordeal by the time the weekend arrived.   He was looking forward to umpiring a table-tennis competition, which Mrs. Bryant had arranged among some of the highly competitive younger members of the youth club. If only the older ones would settle their differences in such a harmless way, he thought.

The tattooed elbow just visible from behind the wall of the centre halted the priest in his tracts. He once again felt vulnerable. People knew where he could be found most of the time. He gave the wall a wide berth, not wanting to be confronted by any surprises.

"Father."

The sound of Spider's voice once again halted the priest in his tracks and he turned to face the youth. The youth was alone and looked around nervously as he beckoned the priest towards him.

"I heard you had some visitors the other night."

The way he spoke made it sound like he had some friends round for coffee.

"I just wanted you to know that I didn't send them round."

"They're part of your group, aren't they?"

The priest was careful not to use the more menacing word 'gang' when he spoke to its members.

"Yes, but I didn't give the order."

"Give the order? Spider, you make it sound like you're fighting a war!"

"They've been dealt with. You won't have any more problems."

He held up a flat hand to emphasize his point and there were fresh cuts on his knuckles. The priest grabbed his wrist.

"Does this always have to be the way you deal with things?"

The question was rhetorical and probably confusing to the youth.

"It's sorted. You won't have any more problems."

Fr. Ryan was not sure if he should thank the youth for his concern, but Spider simply pulled his arm from the priest's grip and walked away. A thank you and an apology in the space of a week! He was privileged! A strange kind of peace poured over the priest. He was now under the protection of Spider and his gang. He felt safe, in an uneasy kind of way.

If reading about the priest's private thoughts made me feel uneasy, reading the next part of the diary made me feel in danger of eternal damnation. It concerned matters that were spoken of inside the confessional box. This was a sacrosanct place. Most priests would rather die than disclose what was said in confession. The teachings of my youth forbade me to read such a thing, yet why would the priest have written it down if not for somebody to read? I pondered the subject for a short time before my curiosity finally won the day.

# CHAPTER 9

Sat. 22nd.

It appeared from the diary that the following incident happened at the end of the weekly session of confessions. The faithful would individually enter a small, dark wooden room, just big enough to kneel down in. There would be very a small window frame, usually meshed, that led to the adjoining room where the priest would sit. A curtain over the mesh on the priest's side would afford a certain anonymity. The penitent would kneel on a hassock and open with the words: 'Bless me father, for I have sinned.' Even outside the confessional, these words meant: 'what I am about to say must not be repeated, discussed or acted upon in any way, with any other person, without my permission.' Confession was used not only to repent, but also to ask for advice on a range of matters. Priests in an open situation regularly give advice, but the option of the confessional box is always there for the more inhibited.

Fr. Ryan listened for a moment, to make certain that nobody else needed to confess. Satisfied that he had completed his work for the evening, he picked up his empty water bottle and his Bible, and stood up. The door in the next room clicked open. The priest sat down again, a little irritated by this latecomer. He was hot and even a little bored at hearing the same sins repeated time after time.

"Bless me father, for I have sinned."

"Then confess your sins and ask for God's forgiveness."

This was one of the three or four replies that the priest automatically gave. He did not even think about it. After thirty seconds of silence, he thought that the man must feel nervous about confessing what he considered to be a grave sin. The priest had heard thousands of sins over the years and felt that he could no longer be shocked, but he decided to give him a little longer to think about it.

"I've lost my faith, father."

This was a common problem that priests often hear and there were standard ways to bring someone back to the fold.

"We all have doubts about our faith sometime in our lives, even catholic priests."

"No father, I don't mean I'm having doubts. I mean that I have found out things that have convinced me that there is no God."

This was far more serious, but the man could not have completely lost his faith or he would not be there in the confessional.

"If you are convinced there is no God, Why have you come to see me?"

"I need your help father."

"I'm always here to help. Any time I have doubts about anything, I pray. The Bible tells us......"

"Why are you quoting the Bible at me?"

The voice was calm and cultured and the priest was taken aback by the question.

"Because it's the word of God. Do you have something to confess?"

"In a way."

"Then ask for God's forgiveness and give yourself some peace."

"I'm going to kill someone."

The priest had heard this claim on a few occasions so it did not shock him. It was usually made as a cry for help by a very distraught person. This man did not seem distraught. His voice was calm and he sounded well educated.

"You know that killing is wrong."

"Why?"

"Because the Bible tells us so."

Was the man trying to claim that he did not know that killing was wrong and therefore he would not be committing a sin if he went ahead? Perhaps he just needed to be told that it was wrong.

"The Bible. Why do you keep quoting ancient history?"

"Because it's the word of God."

"How do you know?"

The priest was not about to get into a theological discussion and decided to reverse the question.

"Don't you believe in the Bible?"

"Of course."

"Why?"

"It's common sense."

"Then you know that killing another human being is wrong."

"In anger, or for personal gain, yes. But this killing isn't for either of these reasons. It will be done out of love. It's a mercy killing. Isn't love what the Bible is all about?"

So this was what the man was talking about. The contentious matter of euthanasia. The church was very clear on the subject.

"Nobody but God has the right to take a life."

"If the core message of the bible is love, then to kill the one you love cannot be a sin if the loving hand commits the deed."

The man was obviously well educated, although quite from what book he was quoting, the priest did not know.

On any other day, Fr. Ryan would have enjoyed a discussion of this nature, but he was tired and the little room was hot and stuffy.

"If you have something to confess, you must show some remorse. If you have come here to get the church to sanction murder, that will never happen. Just why have you come to see me?"

"To tell you that your life could be in danger if you get any more involved in local business."

The man's message was now becoming clear.

"And what gang do you belong to?" Asked the priest with a sigh.

"That doesn't matter, but since you ask, I belong to all the gangs."

This did not make sense, unless he was a lawyer, working for each gang as they approached him. This would explain his calm logical way of thinking, and his level of education. It would also explain why he would not be afraid to be seen in church.

"Father, you're a good man. The people of your church need you here. Don't concern yourself with things you don't understand."

"All of God's children are my concern. Jesus said: "Go ye out and teach all nations...."

"The Bible again. Don't you have any thoughts of your own?"

The priest was now a little irritated, especially because the man was still calm. It was as though the man were talking to a child. However, Fr. Ryan was talking on his own subject and felt that he was more than a match for any lawyer.

"Do you want me to challenge the word of God?"

"No, just to understand it."

This really annoyed the priest but he tried not to let it show in his voice.

"I believe I do understand it. I have a degree in theology."

"And you've learnt nothing!"

Fr. Ryan was no longer prepared to tolerate this tirade of abuse, so he decided to pull rank. After all, he was the priest. Someone who had lived his life by the laws of God. This was a man who defended gangland criminals in court. Someone who twisted laws for his own personal gain. Who was he to interpret the Bible?

"I am a man of God. I live my life according to God's word. You sanction drug-taking, violence and even murder, so how can you say that you understand the word of God better than I do?"

"I don't take drugs or sanction violence. I'm a man of peace."

The man's voice was still calm, even haunting. The priest had gained his second wind by now and was happy to continue this discussion with an intellectual equal.

"It's called collective responsibility," he said. "If you identify yourself with gangs by running messages for them, then you are at least partially responsible for their actions. Haven't you seen the fear and destruction they cause?

"Indeed I have, but I don't understand why you exclude yourself from this. Aren't you a gang member?"

Did this man know about the gun? The priest could not be seen to be taking sides.

"No, I'm not a member of any gang. I talk to all of them but I don't get involved in their affairs. I give them advice and talk to them about Jesus, but I don't sanction their actions."

"Father, you put on a uniform every day, just like they do. You live your life by a code, just like they do. You have regular meetings with likeminded people, just like they do."

He was a clever man, but the priest could see the flaw in his reasoning.

"The difference is that my 'gang' doesn't use violence as a means to an end."

"Religion has used violence as a means to an end for centuries, and still does. Do army chaplains tell the troops not to kill the enemy? Do you not identify with the crusaders by following a code that was acquired through violence? Aren't many modern-day wars fought over religion? Collective responsibility, father!"

The priest was once again getting annoyed, but this time it showed in his voice.

"So what would you have me do? Abandon my religion and join one of your gangs?"

"Father, I didn't come here to argue with you. I came here to ask for your help. I used to be a devout catholic, but now I have lost my faith completely."

"We all have doubts about our faith at one time or another. Have you tried praying?"

"That's the problem. My doubts are about the fundamental principles of faith. I did not slowly drift away from the church, as many people do. My doubts are based on certain information to which I am privy and I have to ask you if you will help me, knowing that I no longer believe the things you believe."

"We are all God's children and I would not be a very good Christian if I turned someone away just because he thinks he has lost his faith."

"I'm relieved to hear you say that, father. It's difficult for me to explain the things I want to tell you because I can't tell you where I got the information. The only thing I can do is to start from the very beginning. I'm going to give you a scenario which might not seem relevant to you at this time, but please bear with me."

He paused briefly to think.

"In a totally hypothetical universe, you are a member of an intergalactic organisation of peaceful planets. You want to expand your membership to other galaxies but you don't want war and violence to mar the peace you have. What do you do? You send down a teacher, a prophet if you like, to set them on the right track. But one prophet wouldn't be enough for such a big world, so you'd send down several, each with the same basic message: love one another and gain a peaceful world. Although the messages would be the same, the way of delivering these messages would vary according to the culture of the country. You'd leave a gap of, say, two thousand years and then you'd send down another group of prophets to teach a more advanced course. This would continue until the aim was achieved and there was world peace. Then the world would gain its prize by being accepted into the organisation, with all the medical and scientific knowledge to enable the people to lead long and happy lives. Now imagine that these prophets returned after four thousand years to give the final lessons, and found that mankind was still arguing about which prophet was right. They found people still dressing-up in ancient robes and sticking rigidly to the ancient laws, without any understanding of why they were made at that time or their relevance to modern-day life. Don't you think they'd eventually decide that this world wasn't worth all the effort, and that they should concentrate their efforts on planets that respond more readily?

"So you think that God is an alien, do you?

This time the man sighed. It was not a sigh of annoyance; more a sigh that one would give a child who had not understood what had just been explained to him.

"Thousands of years of development opportunities and you're still getting bogged down with the wrong questions. It doesn't matter who God is. What matters are his teachings. Going back to the space scenario, would the teachings be in code, so only the learned could understand them, or would they be plain and simple so that everybody could understand? The holy book (whichever one you read) is plain and simple."

"God made the heavens and the earth. He will never abandon us"

"Yes. Isn't it strange that we refer to the galaxy as the heavens? Perhaps there's less of a metaphor there than we think. Open your mind, father."

"You can think of God as an alien if you want, but I know he is our father and that he loves us. Talking about spacecraft is all very fine, but this is a confessional where people come to make their peace with God, not to preach about other faiths. I ask you once again. Why have you come to see me?"

The man's voice was still calm and steady. He did not seem to let anything upset him.

"Father, you're a good man. It's a big world out there and you can't change all of it. The people of your parish need you here. Stick to helping them with the little knowledge you possess, and leave other areas of the community alone. We'll talk again."

With that, the door of the confessional opened again and the priest was alone.

He sat there for a moment, trying to come to terms with what had just happened. He thought that something big must be about to happen if he was being warned off by a lawyer. Was the lawyer a member of his church? So he thought that God was a spaceman! Even so, his message appeared to be one of peace. Would this message change if he did not heed the warning?

Fr Ryan had been trying to help gang members lead a better way of life but he was always treated with mistrust. Now that he had glimpsed the first spark of trust by being given the gun, he could not back off. No, he would continue his work.

He left the confessional and made his way through the back of the church to the parochial house. He had an idea. He opened his writing desk and took out his notebook. This lawyer was educated and connected with the gangs. If he could be taught the true message, and that God wanted him to preach this message, then perhaps Fr. Ryan could begin to teach the word of God by proxy.

The notes that the priest made were not included in the diary, and at this point, I closed it for the night.

I had never imagined a confessional being like this. The man was obviously a little insane, thinking God was an alien, but I hoped I would hear more from him later in the diary.

Alison had finished watching her programme and we went to bed. I had to be fresh in the morning, ready for another week's work.

# CHAPTER 10

I was up bright and early, ready for another day. Alison had cooked my breakfast and made me a packed lunch. I had stopped grinning at the other commuters and instead, adopted a more sombre detached stare, but inside I was still happy. I arrived at work and walked in a side door that led to the room where the kettle was. I was surprised to find it empty. I had never been the first one on site! I wandered through the house and into the back garden, where I saw my workmates talking to the boss. The gloomy looks and the wad of pay packets in his hand told me that it was bad news.

"Now that you're all here," said the boss, "I'm afraid that I have some bad news. My company has been struggling financially these past few months, and now the bank has decided to foreclose on the loans. I'm sorry to have to tell you, but these will be your last pay packets. All work must now stop."

He looked genuinely upset and I almost felt sorry for him, but then I thought of my own situation.

"Where does that leave us?" I asked, even though I knew the answer.

"I'm sorry," was all he could say as he handed me my wages and walked into the house.

We all stood there looking at each other without speaking. Each of us knew how difficult it was to find work. Somebody suggested going for a drink 'to drown our sorrows.' He knew of a bar beside the docks that would be open.

Although we all agreed, I only did so to say goodbye to the people I had been working with. It did not seem right just to walk off site and never see them again. Besides, there was always the chance of meeting someone who knew where there was work.

I was devastated. All our dreams, the plans we had made over the past few weeks were shattered.

While I was with my ex-workmates, things did not seem as bleak. After all, we were all in the same boat. Now that I was alone I felt isolated, cut off from the tide of life like a rock jutting out of the sea, being slowly eroded by the rolling of the waves.

It must have been late afternoon when I climbed the stairs from the tube station into the bright sunshine. I still had to face Alison! I had not had that much to drink but I had not eaten, and it affects me more without food in my stomach. We had spent most of the time talking, and I had learned quite a lot about my workmates. We had even exchanged phone numbers, just in case one of us found a site that needed workers.

I opened the front door and closed it behind me quietly. Perhaps this was to give me a little more time to think about what I was going to say to Alison. She was in the kitchen with Emma and Chloe and she turned when I walked in.

"You're home early," she said with a smile.

The girls came running up to me.

"Daddy," they cried in unison.

I bent down to pick them up, but they caught me off balance as they charged into my arms and I ended up sitting on the floor. This was a source of amusement to us all. Alison offered me a hand and as I got to my feet, she sniffed the air.

"Have you been drinking?" she asked with a concerned look on her face.

Alison knew immediately that something was wrong.

"Go and play in the living room, girls," she said.

Chloe was standing on my feet and Emma had hold of my hand.

"Do as your mother tells you!" I said as I snatched my hand from Emma's grasp.

Heads down, the children made their way quietly to the living room.

"Don't shout at them!" scolded Alison.

"They've got to learn to do as they're told!"

"They usually do if you give them a bit of time. What's the matter with you? What's happened?"

"Work has finished."

"What do you mean finished?  Finished for the day, finished for the week?"

"I mean it's finished!  Finished for good!"

"Don't shout," she said as she closed the door that led to the living room.  "Now tell me what has happened.  How much have you had to drink?"

Was that all she was concerned about?  I had just told her that I no longer had a job, and that was all she could think of to say!

"We were all given our week-in-hand money this morning.  The job has been shut down."

"But I thought you said that he had plenty of work on."

"I thought it would be my fault somewhere along the line!"

"I didn't say that!  Doesn't he have any other sites you could go to?"

"Do you think I'd be standing here if he did?"

She seemed to think that the job had ended and I had not bothered to ask him about other sites. I had not realised she thought I was that casual about work!

"The firm's gone bust. There's no work today, next week or any other week on this, or any other site!"

"I'm sorry, darling. But at least you got two week's wages. You often don't when a company goes bust."

The money. That was all she was worried about. Never mind how I felt, just as long as she got her money!

"You'll get another job. In the meantime, you can sign on. We'll get by. We always have."

She simply did not understand. It was obvious to me now that she did not care that I worked hard all week so that we could have a better life. We were just 'getting by.' Now she was quite happy for me to go and beg the government for money again, so that we could carry on 'getting by.' She had destroyed all the pride I ever had in my work. I felt sick.

"Here's your money," I said as I threw my wage packet onto the worktop.

Alison put on a hurt expression, but it did not stop her from counting the money.

"Have you counted this?" she asked. "It seems a little short."

She obviously did not want me to have any money of my own. I put my hand in my pocket and pulled out some loose change and some screwed-up notes. I put them on the side next to the empty wage packet.

"Here, you might as well have it all! Why should I be entitled to any money when I'm not earning it? I broke into a twenty in the pub. That's the change. I'll owe you the other four pounds something that I spent!"

"I don't care how much you've spent. It's your money. I'm just saying that you're over thirty pounds short in your wages."

"Well I can hardly go back and ask for it now, can I? Unless of course you think that I've spent it!"

"It wouldn't matter if you had spent it. I was only saying you're short, just in case you were looking for it."

She did not believe me. I could tell. I went upstairs for a shower, and then spent the evening reading the paper and watching

TV. I must have dozed off because I do not remember the girls going to bed. In fact, I was so tired that I do not remember going to bed myself.

The following morning Alison woke me with a cup of coffee. It was late and she had already taken the children to school. She sat on the bed beside me.

"How are you feeling?" she asked. The look was almost one of pity.

"Tired, I didn't sleep too well."

"Never mind. I'll make you a nice breakfast while you have a shower. You can't go to the job centre looking like that, can you?"

Why was she treating me like a child? I know when to wash and dress and I know how to look for work.

I washed, dressed, and went straight out. I could not face breakfast anyway, and Alison would only have started another argument. I walked down the road and waited at the bus stop. The bus came after a few minutes and I put my hand in my pocket to get the right change to pay the driver. My pocket was empty. I had forgotten that Alison had taken all my money the night before. I was not going to go back home to beg for pocket money, and have another argument, so I started walking.

It took me a good forty-five minutes to walk to the job centre. I stood there in line one, with all the other hopefuls. The woman behind desk one handed me some forms to fill in.

"If you need help filling them in, go to desk five," she sneered.

I looked at the line of misfits and illiterates in front of desk five. So that was what I looked like to people. I was about to ask her if she could complete the Guardian crossword, but before I could speak another word, she said:

"Next."

Not even a 'please.' People think that I have no brains, just because I am looking for labouring work!

I filled in the forms and queued up again to hand them in. After a few questions, I was told to look at the boards to see if there was anything suitable. I scanned the lists of jobs, my eyes finally settling on the only card that looked even remotely within my sphere of work. Hundreds of trades, full training given, apply now. I read on:

see separate board on H.M. Forces. As I headed for the door, I caught the eye of the woman behind desk one.

"See anything you fancy?"

She still had that sneer on her face, but I was not about to be beaten by her.

"Nothing at all!" I said, as I looked straight into her eyes

I spent the rest of the morning window shopping and sitting in the park, watching the world go by. It was peaceful in the park.

I arrived home at about one o'clock. Alison was vacuuming the living room and did not see me at first.

"You've been a long time," she said when she finally noticed me. "How did you get on?"

"Well there was one job, but it would mean that I would have to join the forces."

Alison laughed.

"You're getting a bit old for that! Look love, I know you're worried about money, but I still have the money my father left me. That'll tide us over until you get another job."

Alison's father and I never got on.  He made no secret of the fact that he thought his daughter could have married someone better than a labourer.  When he died, I told her that the money he left her was hers to do with as she liked.  I wanted nothing to do with it.  Now she was telling me that her dead father could look after my family better than I could.  She certainly knew how to twist the knife!

"That's your money.  I'll get the money to feed my family."

"It's our money," she said.

Not wanting to be drawn into another argument, I went to the bedroom and got out the diary.

# CHAPTER 11

The rest of the diary was undated. There were appointment dates interspersed among the main dialogue, which gave me an idea of the time span between events, but I have simply recorded most of the rest of the events in chronological order.

It was about a week later that the priest talked to the man again. It seems that Fr. Ryan had more contact with the gangs during the week. The diary had brief entries about his having met various gang members, but few details.

"Bless me father, for I have sinned."

The priest immediately recognised the calm, cultured voice in the confessional.

"Ah," he said. "The man who thinks that God is an alien. Have you resolved the other matter yet?"

"What, the killing? It will happen, all in good time."

This time the priest was prepared. He decided to concentrate on the man's promised action, rather than being sidetracked by a theological debate. He had wondered why the man was telling him this if it was going to happen anyway. Perhaps he wanted the gun.

"Who are you going to kill?"

"I can't tell you that father."

"OK. How are you going to kill him?"

"With a stab wound to the heart. It's the quickest way; causes the least pain."

"Why do you want to kill this person?"

"I don't want to kill him. I have already told you, it's an act of mercy."

"All right then, why you and not somebody else?"

The man thought for a moment before he spoke, but his voice did not alter.

"A long time ago, I was in the position whereby I desperately needed help. There were many people around, but only one person willingly helped, and then only in a small way. I will not stand by and see somebody else in that position."

"Tell me, if you're determined to kill this person anyway, why are you telling me about it first?"

"So that you won't think badly of me, father."

"I don't have to think badly about you to think badly about what you intend to do. One can love the person without loving what he does."

Fr. Ryan was pleased at this answer. He had shown Christian love for the man, without condoning his way of life.

"Is a man not the sum of his actions? Don't his deeds live on long after his death? The secret is to understand the reasons behind a person's actions. Then you can love the whole person, not just the parts of his life that conform to some four-thousand-year-old laws to which you stick rigidly. Would you be shocked if I told you that I once knew a man who pointed a gun through the window of another man's house, and shot him through the back of the head, in front of his wife and three children?"

"No. Lawyers meet all kinds of criminals."

"I'm not a lawyer, but it's interesting that you have already condemned this man as a criminal, without knowing anything about him."

"If you're not a lawyer, who are you?  What is your connection with gangland?"

Fr. Ryan was now confused.  He had assumed that the man was a lawyer and that the reason he was telling him these things was so that he could use the priest in some sort of clever defence, if he were ever caught.

"Why do you spend your life asking incidental questions?  It doesn't matter who I am or what my connections are.  Stick to the point.  Why have you condemned this man?"

This was the first time the priest had heard the man raise his voice.  He had only raised it slightly, but it was enough to make Fr. Ryan sit up and listen.

"I don't condemn the man, only his deed.  You told me that he shot the man through the back of the head.  That is a crime against the laws of God as well as the laws of man."

"So what if I now told you that the man in the house was depressed. He had tied-up his wife and children, poured petrol over them and was about to light a match. Also, the police officer who shot him was ordered to do so. It is no longer a crime against man, but it does break one of the commandments, so do you still condemn him?"

"No, of course not. He shot the man to save lives. The act was performed for the good of the man's wife and children. The church allows this. Are you trying to tell me that you think that the Commandments are worthless?"

"Certainly not. They are obviously a very good basic rule. But mankind progressed from those times, over the following two-thousand years. Then came phase two: the New Gospel. Mankind should have had developed enough by that time to have been able to take advantage of this second stage in the plan. 'Turn the other cheek.' This a refinement which can only happen in the later stages of man's development. Jesus said: 'If you ask anything of the Father, you only have to believe that it is yours, and it will be granted to you.' If you want the gangs to become Christian and stop all the trouble they cause, simply ask for it."

"It doesn't work like that. If I ask my heavenly father for something, He will decide whether or not it is good for me before deciding whether or not to grant it."

"That sounds like a get-out clause, to me. Have you ever tried asking Gods from other religions for help?"

"There is only one true God. I will not worship false Gods."

"Quite right. But I can tell you that, no matter which God you ask, the results will be pretty much the same."

"I don't believe that."

"Yes, I understand that, but don't you think that people from other faiths believe the same thing about their Gods?"

"Of course, but they are misguided. They haven't yet heard about Jesus."

"I'm sure that many of them have, but they're quite happy worshiping their 'one true God.' How can humanity ever progress while he adopts this playground, 'my God's better than your God' attitude? Just imagine God coming down to earth to see how mankind had progressed over the last two-thousand years. Imagine a spokesperson from each religion telling him that they have held onto the true faith by trying to convert the others. What do you think his reaction would be?

"You tell me. You still think God is a spaceman!"

The man sighed again. The priest should have known that he would never have got away with such a fatuous comment.

"You're still obsessed by who God is! All right then, we'll take my scenario of the confederation of peaceful planets, which incidentally, is far more plausible than your invisible God who made everything from nothing. The confederation would want mankind to develop in such a way that the nations of the world would all be at peace. Peace can't be forced upon people, and it's no good letting them see the prize. They'd make peace treaties simply to satisfy their greed to gain that prize. And so the federation would have to appeal to whatever was the strongest influence on people's lives: religion! Man has invented Gods since he first saw fire coming out of the ground. As science provided answers to nature and evolution, so the Gods became more intangible, until today when you have only one God who you can't hear, see, feel or touch, that made everything from nothing, in his own image and likeness. Do you realise just how far fetched that sounds? Yet the federation would have used man's insatiable desire for eternal life, as a tool to gain a peaceful world. By the time man's knowledge had increased enough to allow him to rationalise the mysteries of the universe, he would have a peaceful world and his Gods would then be cast into the realms of mythology, like so many others before them."

Fr. Ryan found this theory interesting; wrong, but nevertheless quite compelling.

"Well, it's your theory," he said. "You tell me what went wrong."

"They underestimated man's greed for power. You can't have power over people who think for themselves. You have to give them a common belief, and then adjust the rules to suit your own needs."

"That's a very cynical view on life!"

"You think so? All right then, let me expand that point. You're a Christian and you meet, say, a Moslem. Do you want to kill him?"

"Don't be ridiculous. Of course I don't!"

"Nor he you. So why have Christians and Moslems fought terrible wars over the centuries? Whether it's a nation or a religion, there are always people who want to hijack it for their own personal gains. Most people in the world want to live in peace, but are prevented from doing so by their leaders.

"Yes I can see that, but you can't blame religion for man's greed. Christianity preaches against worldly riches.

"Why then is the Vatican the richest state in Europe, while Italy is one of the poorest?"

"The Vatican has to be self-financing. You can't have the leaders of a state living in abject poverty. They would never be taken seriously."

"Like the prophets, you mean? The point I'm trying to make is that the Bible, from which you seem to like quoting, says quite clearly that killing is wrong. Christ tells us to turn the other cheek, yet you accept that Christian people go out to war with the training and the weaponry to kill people they don't even know, simply because your leaders tell you that God is on their side. Isn't that a bit of an anomaly?"

"I don't condone warfare."

"You don't openly oppose it until it's on your doorstep. Then your leaders say that it's wrong. What would you have these gangs do? Lay down their arms and come to church every Sunday? You have to understand life from their point of view. What are you going to tell them? That Jesus loves them? Most of these people have never had love and if they recognised it at all, it would seem like a weakness.

"I would teach them that God is all powerful. That's something they do understand."

"And when they ask you to prove it?"

"It requires no proof. You have to have faith."

"And what is faith?"

"Faith is a gift from God."

"Am I understanding this correctly? You are going to ask a violent nineteen-year-old youth to pray to an intangible God in whom he doesn't believe, for the gift of faith in order that he might believe in him? Perhaps when he's finished laughing, you could tell him that he would then be able to give up his former life, loose all respect on the streets and stand in the dole queue on a fraction of the money that he could earn running drugs!"

"So what would you have me do? Leave out a whole section of God's children, simply because they're difficult to approach? I am a catholic priest. I can't do that!"

"Father, I admire your strength of faith. Trying to convert the gangs to Christianity will not work and it is also very unwise, especially as it's something for which there is little or no evidence. You base your whole life on a book that was written thousands of years ago. It is a history book, people's interpretations of events which took place at that time. As such, it has to be written from a biased point of view. Anything coming down from the sky at that time would have been interpreted as a God. Try to imagine Christ coming down to Earth today instead of two-thousand years ago. How do you think we would interpret his life? Would we see miracles or trickery? Would we witness the execution of a prophet or of a political agitator in an occupied country? Try reading the Bible as it is, rather than as a convenient interpretation initiated by people with a different agenda.

There are many things that demonstrate extra-terrestrial life forms having been on this planet: cave drawings, ruts forming patterns in the ground which can only be recognised from the air, numerous sightings of u.f.o.'s. The list is endless. Don't you think that if they came this far they would at least have made contact?"

"Are you trying to say that God doesn't exist?"

"I don't know if God exists or not, but I have a shrewd idea who Jesus Christ was from reading about his life. I will say one thing. If God does exist, then it's not his message you've been following all these years."

"So you think that Christ was an extra-terrestrial?"

"Read his life story and judge for yourself. I have to go now, but we will talk again soon and I will explain everything. In the meantime, would you do something for me?"

"If I can."

"I'm going to give you a website address and some pass codes to get into it. Will you look at them?"

"All right."

"Thank you father. They're on a piece of paper, which I'll leave on the hassock. Now I must go."

"Business to take care of?"

The man left the confessional without replying.

I, like many other people, have always had some vague hope of there being life on other planets, but I never considered God's role in all of this. Here were two people discussing the very nature of God!

Alison's family Bible stared at me accusingly from the bedside table. As a child, I had been taught that all the answers were contained within its pages and I wondered if I would find any answers to my life.

I opened it to the gospel according to St. John because I had remembered parts of it from my childhood. Thinking about the words of the man in the confessional, I tried to read it as a history book, substituting the word 'God' for an incorporeal notion of a power outside our existing knowledge, whether natural or otherworldly. I eventually settled on the phrase 'the other world', to make it easier to read.

It began with: 'in the beginning was the WORD', a curious phrase, which appeared to indicate to me that man's faith created

God. I skipped a few pages as I wanted to know what the man meant by reading about the life of Christ to decide whether he was an alien.

I read about the miracles he performed, but decided that a miracle is simply an unexplained event and could equally be performed by a God as by a technologically advanced civilisation. There would be no indication of who he was in his miracles. He was certainly a good man and his teachings were of peace. I reached chapter 11 and read about the raising from the dead of Lazarus. This was something that could only be performed by God. Not even an advanced civilisation has the power over death! It seemed that the man was wrong. Then I read about Christ's trial and subsequent execution. It seemed very odd for a God or an alien not to speak in front of what was essentially a captive audience. He did say that his kingdom was not of this world, perhaps indicating that he was from 'the other world'. His execution however was something that no alien would have endured for a world that was not his own. No, this was definitely a God!

I closed the Bible and replaced it on the table. A rush of guilt flooded over me. I had defiled the holy book with my doubts and I felt empty.

Thinking about how the almighty affects our lives is usually brought home to us in times of trouble. I had abandoned God, abandoned his church, abandoned the teachings of my youth, and now God had abandoned me!

I stood in our bedroom, looking out at the stars through the window and a tremendous feeling of isolation overwhelmed me. Even the stars I could see were billions of miles away through the black, cold void of space. I was alone, spinning on the outside of a small sphere, lost in the vast emptiness of space and time. Nothing I did or was going to do would matter in the grand scheme of things. I had nothing and I was nothing.

I did not turn as Alison entered the room and got ready for bed.

"Coming to bed?" she asked in a way that showed her uncertainty of my mood.

I did not reply. Instead, I turned off the light and got undressed. A burning teardrop etched itself into my cheek like acid, as my misty eyes returned to the blackness outside the window. As I got into bed and felt the warmth of Alison's body next to mine, I realised that I did have something after all. I clung tightly to her as a drowning man clings to a life raft, and told her that I loved her. A simple kiss on the cheek from this marvel of a woman, and all the fear and desolation that I was feeling, slowly ebbed away. I do not believe that I released my grip on her all night.

# CHAPTER 12

The daily routine of visiting the job centre, only to see the disappointment in Alison's face when I returned, did little to ease the tension at home.  When the weather was good, I would take the diary and sit on a park bench, preferring to read about the life of the priest than to face the looks of pity reflected in the faces of my family.  If I sat around the house reading, Chloe would always want something or Alison would want to vacuum in whatever room I was in.  Basically I was just in the way.  So, it was on a pleasant Thursday morning that I chose a shady spot in the park and sat on a bench, enjoying the peace and quiet.

I did not notice her at first as she moved very slowly, bent over her walking stick. The long checked coat swamped her slight frame and the round blue hat made her a figure from a former century. I watched as she shuffled past me, her face rutted by the years, was fixed in concentration on the path ahead as she undertook her epic journey step by step.

It seemed to happen in slow motion; her trailing foot slid level with the other, bouncing against the rough tarmac, and the body, leaning forward in anticipation of a step, spiralled round the stick ever downward. I found myself on my feet, my hands clamped around her upper arms and in that split second I was torn between slowing her decent and not injuring her. My knees were bent, supporting her body and even through her thick coat, my hands almost surrounded her upper arms. I eased my grip a little and encouraged her to her feet. I could have lifted her onto the bench without any effort but instead she held my hand for support as she eased herself into a sitting position.

"Thank you so much," she said after she got over her momentary shock.

I think I had probably suffered almost as much a shock as she had. My heart was still racing and adrenalin was making my hands tremble.

"Are you all right?" I asked.

An ancient hand patted the back of mine and in that instant I felt a link to another century. A lifetime of knowledge and experience went into that simple act and I noticed my body had stopped trembling and I felt more at peace than I had felt in years.

"I'm all right, thanks to you. It must be wonderful to be big and strong and be able to help people. People like you make the world a better place to live in."

I was a little overawed at this synopsis of my life from someone who hardly knew me and I felt that I could not lay claim to such a tribute.

"You wouldn't say that if you saw me in a rugby match," I said, trying to set the record straight.

"Oh rugby's just a game," she replied dismissively. "Out here in the real world is where it counts. You can't hide your true nature. When I fell, you caught me. You didn't think about it, your inner self, your true nature made you help rather than stand back and watch another human being hurt. That is the sign of a good person."

Her body might have suffered the ravages of time, but her eyes were bright, alert, searching into my very soul. This frail woman held a gentle power that I had never before experienced.

"We're all born with a knowledge of the basic morals of life. It's only our upbringing that reinforces or destroys this."

"But I thought that morals were taught. I certainly teach them to my two girls."

"Yes, and I'm certain you teach them very well. Most parents teach their children not to steal, lie, fight with other children etc. but these are not morals in themselves, they are the products of morals, a reflection if you like of your everyday life. If one of your daughters paints you a monstrosity of a picture and tells you it's a house, you're not going to tell her it looks nothing like a house, are you?"

I remembered the last picture Chloe painted. Promising to hang it on the wall after she had gone to bed, Alison and I spent most of the evening trying to work out which way up it was so that Chloe was not disappointed the next morning. As ever, Alison being the brains of the family suggested that we told Chloe that we could not hang it until she wrote her name **at the bottom**.

"What lengths would you go to, to protect your children? If they were starving and there was no other way, would you not steal food for them? If they were in danger, would you not fight to protect them?"

"Yes, of course I would. I'd die for them."

"Your family doesn't need you to die for them; it needs you to live for them. Morals cover all aspects of life, not just fair weather days."

"Then how would you define a moral?" I asked, intrigued by this gentle person who seemed to have all the answers.

"Morals, my dear, are a hierarchy of responsibilities in life."

She patted my hand again as if to reinforce her point.

"Your first responsibility is towards your children, to protect and teach them so that they will have a good life. A product of this moral is that in everyday life neither you nor they accept such behaviour as lying, stealing or fighting. Conversely, in exceptional circumstances, that same moral not only allows, but compels you to break one or all of these rules. The moral still stands while the circumstances and the reaction to these circumstances changes.

Everybody has to decide for himself what this hierarchy is, but the person who sticks to his morals, doesn't have any anomalies in life. The rest is just common sense. We all want to live in a peaceful world so we discourage fighting, stealing etc."

She removed from her pocket a clear plastic bag containing a small quantity of crumbed bread, and placed it on my lap.

"Would you be kind enough to feed the birds for me?" she asked as she eased herself to her feet. "I usually feed them at this time of day but now I have to go."

And so she tottered off leaving me to shower the ground with crumbs for the ravenous sparrows.

I sat there for a moment, watching the birds pecking at the last few morsels as I mulled over what the lady had said. I could not refute her theories but decided that life was a little more complicated than she had painted it.

Screwing up the plastic bag and depositing it in the bin beside me, I returned to the diary.

# CHAPTER 13

The priest had picked up the website addresses and passwords from the confessional. He seemed to be more interested in the man and from where he was getting his information, then in the actual information itself. If he could find an inroad into this man's way of thinking, perhaps he could use it to his advantage.

He had accessed the relevant information when he was disturbed by a parishioner knocking on the door. He pressed the download button and left the computer to do the work.

There was no mention in the diary of what the parishioner wanted, but it was an hour or so later that the priest returned to the website. He wrote parts of what he read in the diary, but it was difficult for me to decipher. It seemed to contain military reports of alien landings and other contacts with extra-terrestrial beings. It mentioned a race called the Jawehens, which apparently was not the same race as Gen.1 or JC. but the same organisation. The notes were difficult to read and made no sense to me at the time. The report was dated 1948 and the race was apparently peaceful, but a recommendation to implement the Star-Wars project was made, in the interests of global security. The diary also had the words: 'Contact MIR urgently' with a big question mark after it. This obviously made no sense to the priest either.

The diary continued later that night with the priest being woken by a loud banging on the door. He slipped-on his dressing gown and walked, bleary-eyed towards the front door. He hesitated, checking that the chain was on, not wanting a repetition of previous late-night calls. He opened the door a fraction, keeping his foot behind it as added security.

"Police," said one of the three, well-dressed men that met his gaze. The man was holding a card in his hand but the lateness of the hour and the dim lighting prevented the priest from reading it.

"Police, at this time of night! What do you want?"

"Fr. Ryan?" said the smallest of the three, almost rhetorically.

"Yes." The priest's eyes had now fully opened and his mind had disentangled itself from his dreams.

"We need to speak to you. Can we come in?"

"Just a moment," said Fr. Ryan as he closed the door a little to undo the chain.

He wondered whom he would have to bail out of trouble this time. Would it be Spider again?

He opened the door once again and led the officers into the living room. He beckoned them to the chairs, but they remained standing. He had often noticed this about the police. They reminded him of a puppy he had when he was a child, wandering around the room, sniffing in every corner, investigating everything within the range of senses. But the next comment was something for which he was not prepared.

"May we have the firearm please father?"

He felt the blood drain from his face. How did they know about the gun? This could be dangerous. The police knew that he has a gun, but he dared not tell them where he got it. Spider and his gang would know about the police coming around. It was their business to know these things. He had been given the gun in confidence and would not betray that trust, but would they know that? Just how much did the gangs trust him? Was it one of the gang members who betrayed him? It must have been, how else would they have found out? He wanted to stall but could not think of anything to say.

"Firearm?" he said, trying to look puzzled.

The man held his hands about six inches apart, palms facing each other.

"You know," he said laconically. "About so long, barrel, trigger, used for shooting people."

The priest could not plead ignorance any longer.

"Oh the gun! How did you find out about that? I was going to hand it in tomorrow, but now you've saved me the trouble."

"It's not quite as simple as that," said the officer. "Would you mind coming down to the station with us to answer a few questions?"

That was the other thing he had noticed about the police. They never answered questions, only asked them.

One of the other officers guided the priest towards the passageway door.

"If you wouldn't mind getting dressed now father."

Fr Ryan went upstairs to get dressed. What had he got himself into? He was now on the brink of being a criminal and he longed for the safety of his former life. He wanted to be at peace with everyone, yet he was now in trouble with the gangs and the police. Where had it all gone wrong? The bishop would have to be informed. 'Oh Lord,' he thought, 'the bishop!' Every time he met the bishop, he felt as though he was being called to the headmaster's office. Quite how the bishop would cope with this, he had no idea!

He put on his coat and walked back into the living room. As he turned off the light and accompanied the officers to their car, he wondered what fate was awaiting him.

The short journey to the police station was made in silence. The streets were almost empty as the car sped its way through the night, occasionally lighting-up an odd suspicious character who would turn his face from the brightness of this intrusion. Even when the officers were buzzed through reception, not a word was spoken.

Only when they reached the open door of a cell, was the silence broken.

"We'll just pop you in here for a while, father," said the tall officer. "It'll save you any embarrassment. It could get quite busy here later on."

Fr. Ryan meekly walked into the cell and heard the heavy door close behind him. He had been in cells before when he had visited various members of the local youth, but the door had always been left open. Now that he was trapped in this small room with its meagre furniture and glass-blocked window, he had a sudden impulse that he wanted to be free. This, he thought was irrational as he would be asleep if he had been at home. He could sleep just as well here. He lay down on the thin mattress and shut his eyes, but his mind remained wide-awake and after a few moments, so did his eyes. Pictures of the bishop, a grey man with weaselly eyes, kept flashing into his mind. He hated being frightened of his boss, and of the unchristian thoughts he felt every time they met. They were, after all, on the same side: the side of God.

The priest knelt down and prayed for some solution to the mess that he was in. God knew that he had only good intentions in the things he was trying to do. Perhaps he had been naïve, stupid even, but he was trying to do the Lord's work and God would forgive his failings and release him from his captors. As if in answer to his prayers, the cell door opened and a plain-clothed officer whom he had not previously met, stepped into the room.

"Would you like to come with me, Father," he said softly but firmly. The priest looked for some expression on the officer's face as an indication of the gravity of the situation, but there was none. These people really knew their jobs!

The officer led him into an interview room and they sat down at opposite sides of a small table.

"Who gave you the gun?" he asked without any other formalities.

The priest was shocked by the suddenness of the question, even though he had expected it. He tried to remember the reply that he had formulated in his mind.

"I'm sorry officer but I can't tell you that. It was handed to me in confidence."

"Under the seal of the confessional, I suppose."

Fr. Ryan could have taken the easy way out and said yes, but his mind was drawn to the trial of Christ, and he felt that he could not lie.

"Not exactly," he replied, expecting the officer to pounce on his answer.

"It doesn't matter, we know where it came from."

This comment was not what the priest was expecting. How did he know where it came from? Who had betrayed both him and the gangs? Could it have been the man in the confessional? He would have had no reason to go to the police, but neither would any of the gang members! Everybody knew the rules and the consequences of breaking them. Yet somebody had broken them. Somebody was playing a very dangerous game for whatever reason, and he was right in the middle!

"You know that it is a very serious crime to have an unlicensed firearm in your possession?"

"Of course," said he priest, "but I was going to hand it in. I'm on your side, officer. I saw the opportunity to get a gun off the streets and I took it. I was doing your job for you. Surely you don't think that I am a criminal!"

The faint hint of a smile briefly flickered across the face of the officer.

"No father, I don't think that you're a criminal, but I do think that you're getting involved in things that are, shall we say outside your particular field of expertise."

He seemed to be choosing his words very carefully.

"I'll make a deal with you father. I won't preach the word of God if you don't get involved in my field of expertise. We all have parts of our lives that we would prefer not to have aired in public, even catholic priests. I'm sure I won't have to talk to you on this subject again. If you wait there for a minute, an officer will give you a lift home."

The priest felt that he had just been threatened, without knowing the form of the threat. As the officer stood up to leave the room, Fr. Ryan asked the question that had been most preying on his mind.

"Have you contacted the bishop?"

Once again a faint flicker of a smile flashed across the face of the officer.

"I'm sorry father, we had to."

The officer left the room and Fr. Ryan sat there stunned. Not only had they contacted the bishop, but they had woken him up! The priest was trying to decide whom he feared the most: the gangs, the police or the bishop. I think in the end, the bishop won by a long staff!

The night streets looked different on the way home, somehow more dangerous. He had worried about going to the police station and getting into trouble with the bishop, but after he was dropped-off and the car drove away, he felt a very strong sense of vulnerability. The twenty or so steps up the gravel path that led to his front door seemed to take forever. Once through the gate in the tall privet hedge, every bush and shrub seemed to hide a shadowy figure lurking in the darkness, watching, ready to pounce. The sound of his steps had doubled in volume and echoed against the flint building. A noise behind him halted the priest in his tracks. It was only a faint sound of movement but it was very close. Fr. Ryan froze, resigning himself to whatever fate awaited him. Would they ask him first what he had told the police, or would they simply assume and exact a gangland revenge? Would he be able to convince them that he had not betrayed them, even if they did ask? He prayed silently and earnestly for his ordeal to be over.

The gravel moved behind him and he turned, reasoning that it would be better to face his adversary than to be accosted from behind. He could see no one, the narrow path was clear. The gravel moved again, and as he looked down, his eyes fell on the small prickly creature, going about his nightly business, completely oblivious to any of the fear and trepidation he was causing. Fr. Ryan's body was trembling and his hand shook so much that he could hardly get the key in the lock. Once inside, he leant with his back against the closed door and thanked God for delivering him from yet another crisis. He did not get much sleep during what remained of the night.

I closed the diary at this point and stretched out my body in the sunlight. The position the priest had got himself into made my meagre problems pale by comparison. He had his faith to keep him going, just like Alison. What did I have? I had Alison and the girls, but they had their religion to cling to; they had their own lives of which I was no part. Perhaps I should pray for a job. It seemed to work for Fr. Ryan, but then, he was a priest and had a hotline to the almighty. Why would God listen to me? I did not even go to church!

I looked up into the blue skies, squinting against the sun's strong rays. The view was far removed from that of the previous night, yet I knew that the stars were still there, that there was still a dark, cold void. Yet somehow the world was more peaceful in the sunlight, even though I knew that it was just a façade. I thought about the house I had been renovating. The walls were still the same, yet with a bit of render and a splash of paint, the whole building could be transformed. Perhaps the whole of life was a façade and it did not matter what a person believed in, just as long as he believed that there was something he could turn to that would protect him in times of need.

This seemed to me to be a very cynical point of view, so I developed it further in my mind.

What in our lives was not a façade? If a man bought a new car, only to find it had a slight dent in the wing, would he not return it, demanding a perfect model? Yet the car would perform its function equally well with or without a dent. Even the car being the wrong colour would meet with remonstrations. Everything in life had to appear better than it was and what were originally regarded as extras, then took on a precedence of their own, even down to the houses we live in and the clothes we wear. Perhaps our Gods have developed in the same way, from spitting fire out of the ground to creating the entire universe. Yet people who follow their own religions, seemed somehow to be more at peace with the world. Not all religions can be right, but they appear to have the same effects on those who believe. I wonder if the faithful know this in the same way that they know that fashion is someone else's opinion of what they should wear, but carry on regardless, reasoning that it is their choice of what is right? Did God turn Fr. Ryan's would-be assailant into a hedgehog, did he cut the interview with the police short? I suppose it depends by which façade you live your life. The biggest façade of all, of course, was life after death. We see people die, we see them interred or cremated, no longer the person we knew but an organic compound ready to be broken down to basic elements in order to reconstitute into other life forms. Yet religion tells us that there is this invisible thing called a soul that only man has, and it is this intangible thing that lives on in a place called heaven. That must be bad luck for animal lovers. God is apparently quite happy to let his beloved people die horrendous deaths for not recanting this belief!  What fear people must have of religion, to be able to bear such ordeals, sanctioned by a God who purports to love them!  No, I will not pray to any God for work.  I might as well pray to the bench I am sitting on!

I sat there and uttered a silent prayer to the park bench, just to reinforce my theory.  But could I live within the bounds of religion?  Would that bring me closer to Alison and the girls?  I would not have to change very much, just go to church with them and offer the occasional 'Thank God' when something went according to plan.  I would not have to have my faith tested by ordeal!  But could I live under this pretence?  My mind then returned to the analogy of the renovated house, and I realised that I was already living under a fragile veneer that would disintegrate if any part of it were damaged.  That was why the smallest things were so important.  Perhaps I would give religion another try.

The journey home from the park gave me more time to reflect on my theories.  I saw a woman sweeping her pathway, trying to make it look as if it had never been dirty.  The clean-cut hedges surrounding the gardens and the knife-edged flower beds were surely not as nature had intended them to be.

The bus hit traffic just before going under a bridge. High on the wall of the bridge clung a little purple flower, insignificant in itself, but nevertheless part of the miracle of life that goes on all around us. The tiny flowers struggled to keep their heads up and some of the leaves had been scorched by the sun, but the plant took on a beauty all of its own. There was no pretence here, this was real! But then, man had no active part in its life and, I realised that, left to itself, nature created far more beauty than man could ever hope to achieve. I found myself hoping that God would protect this little plant, and something inside me knew that he would. This religion thing was becoming easy to fall back into!

As I walked in the house, I kissed Alison on the cheek. This seemed to surprise her, but not in an unpleasant way.

"How did you get on today?" she asked.

"No jobs today, but there's always tomorrow." I said, trying to sound cheerful. "Don't worry, God will provide for us."

Her silence was deafening as I walked into the living room and hugged my children.

Placing all my troubles into the hands of another, however insubstantial, seemed to relieved me of a great burden. Unlike the priest, I was not being chased by ruthless criminals or the police, and to be honest, life was ticking over quite well. My transition into this protective state was a little anomalous to Alison at first, especially when I suggested that I might accompany them to church on Sunday, but she handled it well. She even told me that it was nice to see me smiling again. I had not realised that I had stopped!

# CHAPTER 14

The sneering look of the girl behind desk one, or the lack of suitable employment couldn't dull my mood the next day as I left the misnomer of a job centre and headed for the park. I settled down on my favourite bench and opened the diary.

The next entry was a few days later, when Fr. Ryan booted up his computer. With all that had gone on in the previous few days, he had forgotten about the man in the confessional. He had met agnostics before, but never one with the in-depth knowledge and theories of this man. Perhaps the data he had downloaded would help him to understand where the man had gone wrong, and then maybe he could help him to find the truth. It would also divert the priest's mind from his troubles.

He clicked on the file to open it and a box came up saying 'open pictures now'. He thought he might see pictures of alien beings, genuine or not, but nothing could have prepared him for what he did see. There was picture after picture of children, naked children in compromising positions with adults! The shock of this made the priest panic and he pressed the 'off' button on his computer, not caring about shutting it down properly. He felt sick and went to the sink, retching before shakily drinking a glass of water. This was not the file he had been reading a few nights before. Maybe he had clicked on the wrong file, but what was that filth doing on his computer? He had heard of people being able to hack into computers and download all kinds of things, but this!

The phone rang and Fr. Ryan wiped his mouth before answering it. It was the bishop's secretary, telling him that he had an appointment so see the bishop on the following Tuesday. He pointedly refused to say why the bishop wanted to see him. The priest wondered if anything else could possibly go wrong. Where had his serene life disappeared to? Prior to this, his biggest problems had been trying to reschedule appointments and, of course, the three-monthly meetings with his boss! Now he had child pornography on his computer, he was in trouble with the police, the bishop, the gangs on the streets and on top of that, he may have evidence of an alien race that have not yet heard of Jesus! A section of God's creation that had the right to know about the saviour.

As he walked back from the telephone table, he happened to glance out of the window. There was a man sitting in a car opposite who seemed to be watching the house. The fat, bald man looked away when he saw the priest looking at him, but kept glancing shiftily over his newspaper as Fr. Ryan kept watch. He wondered if it was the man from the confessional, the one who must have betrayed him.

He went out to the kitchen for a drink, as his mouth was still dry from the shock of the photos .It was then that he noticed the note that had been posted through his door. He had not noticed it the night before, or when he got up that morning but the brown envelope blended in well with the mat, so it could have been posted any time. He picked it up and walked to the window. If the fat man knew that he had found it, he might go away.

The man still sat in his car casting furtive glances in the priest's direction. Fr. Ryan sat down and opened the envelope. The note simply said that the passwords had been changed and it also gave another website address and more pass codes. He dared not turn on his computer again, let alone download anything. He put the note away safely. He would have to go to the centre soon, although he could phone with an excuse. No, that would only be putting-off the inevitable.

He put on his coat and left the house. As he walked out of the gate, he got a better look at the fat man and noticed that he was wearing a tie. He was definitely not a gang member! That only left the man in the confessional.

It was a short walk to the centre, but to the priest, every step could be fraught with danger. Everybody he saw looked suspicious and he was sure he was being followed, but despite glancing over his shoulder on numerous occasions, he saw nothing unusual.

He walked into the centre, waved a greeting to Mrs. Bryant who was dealing with a new membership, and went to make himself a cup of tea. A tattooed hand shot out from the storeroom and grabbed him by his upper arm, pulling him inside. Spider shut the door and confronted the priest.

"You're in a lot of trouble father," he whispered.

"Look Spider," said the priest, "I had to give the gun to the police. They knew that I had it, but I didn't mention any names. They told me they knew where it came from, but I didn't tell them, and I made sure that I wiped any prints off first."

The priest was terrified. He had not realised just how frightening a figure this fit young man could be, muscles bulging, face intense.

"Yes I know that," whispered Spider. "They don't know where it came from. They were just bluffing. They don't care about the gun."

"Well that's good!" said the priest as he breathed a sigh of relief.

"No it ain't good," said Spider emphatically. "If they're not interested in the gun, that means that they're interested in something bigger! What else did plod ask you about?"

The priest was now totally baffled. He thought that he was in trouble with the gangs, but it seemed now that the gangs were trying to warn him.

"Believe me, Spider, if there was anything else I would tell you. I don't know what's going on. There was a man watching my house earlier on. I have no idea who he's working for or what his interest is in me."

"He's plod, he followed you here" said Spider nonchalantly. "Not local though. Neither were the three who picked you up."

"They took me to the local police station."

"Yea, but I bet they hid you well. They ain't drug squad and they ain't C.I.D.

"Well who are they then?" asked the priest, wondering how everybody he spoke to on the matter seemed to know far more than he did.

Spider shrugged.

"Could be porn squad. What did it say on their card?"

Fr. Ryan looked sheepish as he admitted that he had not actually read the identity card, especially after all the advice he had given to people on the subject.

"Don't worry," said Spider. "We'll sort it. Anything you need, just ask."

"Look Spider, I don't want to be the cause of you getting into trouble."

"Why not?" said the youth. "Make a change to have a good reason. What do you need?"

Fr. Ryan could not remember the last time he had seen Spider smile, but he had certainly never seen him wink before.

"There's something wrong with my computer and I need to download some files from the web."

"Oh, you need an untraceable line," he replied as if he knew exactly what the priest wanted. "I'll sort it but you got to be ready at short notice. Carry a disk and any website addresses you need with you at all times."

"Thanks Spider. It's not pornography," he said defensively.

Spider just shrugged his shoulders.

"None of my business," he said as he disappeared out of the back door.

The deeper in trouble the priest got, the better I felt about my own life. I still went to the job centre every weekday, but I now felt better because it was not my fault that I was out of work. This is probably the same reason that people pass-on malicious gossip or crowd around accident scenes. Seeing or hearing about a person in unfortunate circumstances, increases the gap of the comparatives by which we live our lives. It is like a manager in a company who, realising that he will not be promoted, employs under-managers. Even though his position is the same, it can now be re-defined as being in charge of other managers. Instead of climbing the ladder of success, he has simply added a few metres to the base. God's will may seem strange to us at times, but I felt sure that the omnipotent had a plan for me. Feeling that the big boss had such a plan, made me feel far more important than I felt as a struggling job seeker. I was beginning to understand religion, and it worked!

I did start going to church with my family and I was amazed how the responses to the prayers came flooding back. The priest was happy to see me but Alison was still a little suspicious.

"You don't have to come to church with us tomorrow," she said one Saturday night.

I was doing the wrong thing again. I thought she would be pleased!

"Don't you want me to go?" I asked indignantly.

"Of course I do," she said. "I just don't want you to feel that you have to."

I seemed to be the only one making an effort in this relationship. I was trying hard to fit into the religious part of her life but she did not seem to care about all my efforts. First, she wanted me to go to church, now she wanted me to go for the right reasons. What are the right reasons? Did everybody who attended mass on a Sunday do so for the right reasons?

"I don't feel that I have to go," I replied. "I want to go."

"Why now, all of a sudden?"

Alison's attitude seemed a little obtuse to me. Perhaps she did not want me to go; perhaps somehow I embarrassed her by going. Was I encroaching on a part of her life that she wanted to keep to herself, hidden from me? Was I preventing her from socialising with her church friends, or were some of the relationships closer than I would have liked? I had not thought of this and I did not want to believe that Alison would do such a thing but I often heard that the husband is always the last to know! I would definitely be going to church with them this Sunday!

I did not want another argument so I just muttered something about finding God and then switched-on the TV.

# CHAPTER 15

The next day in church, I was on my best behaviour. I had put on a jacket and managed to find a tie. I had even washed the car!

It was a very strange feeling being in a church again. Not unpleasant at all and somehow even peaceful. I began to notice things that I remembered from my childhood: the statues, the Stations of the Cross that told the story of Christ's passion pictorially along the two longer walls. Even without the incense, churches have a smell all of their own. They seem to take on the odour of all the past ceremonies that had occurred within their walls.

The prayers had altered little since my childhood and I gave the responses loud and clear with very few mistakes. The hymns of course had not changed and it felt good to sing and relive some of my childhood memories.

It was not such a bad thing being here and at least Alison would be pleased.

After mass that day was the first time I talked to the priest without any pangs of guilt. He remarked at how good it was to see me here with my family.

Alison had just finished talking to one of the other women when I noticed a short, slim, slightly effeminate looking man heading in her direction. He was immaculately dressed and as he approached my wife with arms outstretched, he kissed her on the cheek.

The man obviously had not seen me and, taking my leave of the priest, I took my place at Alison's side.

"Hello darling," he said.

So this was the man who was trying to make a move on my wife. He was about five feet three and by the look of his carefully manicured hands, he had never done a days' work in his life. He was the kind of person that Alison's father would have wanted her to marry. He probably owned a big house and went down well at the local golf club. He even picked up one of the girls with the familiarity of a man who thought he had his feet firmly under the table. He had not noticed me and I felt my muscles tighten and my chest puff out as I stepped forward to be introduced. He handled the introduction well and even remarked on what a big 'chap' I was.

"You have a lovely family here," he said, smiling in an ingratiating way.

"Yes, and I intend to keep them!" I replied tersely.

This ended the conversation and the man made his excuses and left. I had put him in his place and I would not have to worry about him again.

The journey home was made in silence. Even the girls could tell that their mother was in a bad mood. What had I done this time? I had been trying really hard, going to church, joining in with the ceremony and I had stopped this little maggot of a man from pestering my wife. I had done everything a wife could possibly ask of her husband. Why was she being so ungrateful?

A tense atmosphere ensued for the rest of the day but it was not until late evening when the girls were tucked-up in their beds, that the subject was broached. It was again Alison who started the argument.

"Do you enjoy embarrassing me in front of my friends?" she asked.

I did not know what she was talking about, or why she was trying to start an argument.

"You've been in this mood all day."

"That's hardly surprising!" she said. "Embarrassing me in front of everybody like that!"

"Like what?" What have I done to embarrass you?"

"Do you think that blurting out prayers ahead of everyone else makes you look holier than them? And the way you treated Nigel!"

"Nigel?"

"You remember Nigel? The one you almost pummelled into the ground!"

"Oh, the little creep who was trying to get his feet under the table. How did you expect me to react? Did you think I'd just stand there and play happy families?"

"You'd have to learn what a happy family is first!" she said as she walked out of the room and slammed the door.

This last comment threw me. So, Alison was unhappy with me. Perhaps she preferred Nigel the creep, to a real man! I wondered just how long this relationship had been going on. It is funny how fathers live on in their daughters.

Not wanting any further arguments, I got out a rugby video and settled down for an evening's entertainment. I knew I would not be disturbed for the rest of the evening.

I could not concentrate on the video. My mind kept going over what Alison had said.

This was not how it was supposed to have worked! I had gone back to my religion, yet it was causing problems in my life. I considered that perhaps God was working against me, paying me back for years of religious neglect. Perhaps he was punishing me for reading about the confessional and threatening me not to continue!

Whether propounded by man or God, threats always bring out the worst side of my character. I would continue to read the diary, even though I knew that this was one fight that I could never win.

# CHAPTER 16

The days passed and I regularly found myself sitting in the park. Sometimes I would read the diary, sometimes I would simply watch the world go by. I often thought of the old lady and wondered if I would ever meet her again. With her advanced years, I supposed that she would see life as being simple, looking at it from a somewhat retrospective point of view. I wondered just how well she would cope with my particular situation. She would probably tell me to go to church and pray for help. I was feeling a little ambivalent towards religion after my last failed attempt, but it did seem to work for some people. Perhaps she could tell me what was lacking in me to make it work.

The park was empty except for the occasional person rushing through to keep some important appointment or other, so I opened the diary and deciphered a few more pages.

Fr. Ryan scanned the road as he shut the gate behind him. The fat policeman was still sitting in his car, but another figure, much larger and bulkier was leaning against a tree across the road. Donkey was talking to some of his mates and did not appear to notice the priest.

As he walked on, he heard a car door slam behind him. Was the man following him? There was a white van parked about fifty yards ahead and the priest decided to stand behind it, to see if the man would walk past.

Fr. Ryan was parallel with the white van when the sliding door opened and he was bundled inside. The van smelled of oil and of the four men he had vaguely made out before the door closed.

"Got the disk with you, father?" said an unfamiliar voice.

The priest assumed that this was Spiders doing but he was concerned at the newfound popularity he was gaining outside his house.

"Yes, I've got everything I need. I have to tell you, though, that I'm being followed."

"Not anymore," said another unfamiliar voice and they all laughed.

The journey seemed an endless trial of being bumped and jostled. It was dark and he would not have been able to see his travelling companions even without the thick sweet-smelling smoke that hung in the air like liquid silk. He was beginning to feel light headed from inhaling it and politely refused the offer by one of the men, of a 'direct feed'.

He was sitting on something hard and flat, with his legs crushed up against a heavy lump of metal that smelt like a car engine.

The men were talking in short bursts of words in a language that the priest eventually decided was very much like English. Nothing that was spoken made any sense to him, but perhaps that was the idea.

As the van finally came to a halt at the end of a short, bumpy track, he felt a canvas bag being pulled over his head.

"This is for your own good father," said one of the men.

The priest was led out of the van and into a building where he was told to wait. A sudden thought hit him. If these men were not acting on Spider's behalf, he could be in serious trouble because this looked horribly like an execution!

After a few minutes, one of the men returned and led the priest down some steps and into another room. The man stood behind him and removed the bag.

"Take your time father. When you've finished, press the buzzer on the wall and stand facing away from the door."

The priest nodded. Somehow, he knew that he should not look around until he heard the door shut.

The room was small with one central light. The walls were rendered with a thin coat of white paint over the top and the uneven low ceiling made it look somewhat like a cave. There were no windows and only the high-Tec electronic gadgetry that covered every shelf, table and bookcase in the room told the priest that he was not really in a dungeon. He sat down on the only chair in the room, in front of the computer, the only gadget that he could identify. He inserted the disk and typed in the web address. The speed of this machine was phenomenal! Almost as soon as he pressed the return key, the boxes came up saying 'please enter security code.' He put in the codes and downloaded to disk. Thirty seconds later, he was entering the second set of codes.

It was then that the gravity of the situation really hit him. What was he doing here? What did he hope to achieve. Spider was certainly right about his being in trouble, but with whom? The police had let him go with just a warning, although they were still keeping an eye on him so he was not in trouble with them. The gangs on the street seemed to be on his side and the man in the confessional, although acting as a spokesman for the gangs and appearing to be warning him off them, did not seem to pose any threat. Why would Spider have helped him if he wanted him out of the way? With whom then was he in trouble? A pallid, weaselly face flashed into his mind as he remembered his appointment with the bishop. But Spider would not consider the bishop to be a threat and he would not use the phrase 'a lot of trouble' lightly. This was a young man who described being arrested for violent assault as 'a little bit of bother.' Here he sat, a catholic priest in an illicit den, downloading information that he was certain he should not have access to.

He sat for a moment, reflecting on what he had done and the choices he had made. Firstly, everything he had done was for the good of mankind. Of that, he was certain. A man had come to him claiming that he had evidence of God's people in need of help. If the information he had downloaded proved this, the church would have to act and he would be relieved of the burden of this knowledge. He would confront the bishop with this information and perhaps that would make him a little more understanding over the gun incident. The word 'understanding' did not seem to go with that grey face and Fr. Ryan hoped that the disk would contain overwhelming evidence of the alien life forms.

He put the disk in his pocket and pressed the buzzer. Then he stood with his back to the door, waiting like a condemned man for the hood to be placed over his head.

The journey home was much the same as the journey there. It was mainly held in silence and the priest sat with his arms on his knees, looking at the floor. Although there was little light, he did not want the men to think that he could possibly identify them. The van dropped him off near some waste ground at the back of the church and he stepped out. He heard the door slide shut and the van drive away, but he never looked around.

A shadow passed over the book. At first I thought it was a cloud, but then it returned to cover the page once again. I looked up through the eyes and into the archival mind of the old woman.

"Hello again," she said pleasantly. "Do you mind if I join you?"

"Of course not."

I stood up and offered my arm in support. She sat down and adjusted her attire before she spoke.

"I've just been to the church to wish my Bert a happy birthday. He would have been ninety-three today."

This opening statement threw me. Perhaps this would not be the best time to mention my feelings on religion, so I tried the sympathetic approach that I thought she needed.

"I'm sure you'll see him again in heaven, one day."

The response was not what I was expecting.

"Oh I don't believe in all that nonsense. All this heaven and hell business with God reigning supreme, grovelling on your knees to one who is supposed to love you....."

"But I thought you said you'd just been to church."

"Yes I have. I like being in church. I like the singing, the people there and it's where I said goodbye to Bert."

Tact has never been my strong point and I felt awkward asking the next question.

"I thought that all people from your time were religious."

That could have come out better but it seemed to amuse the old lady. She laughed.

"You mean that because I'm so old, I should be cramming for my final exams, just in case there is a God?"

Now I was really embarrassed and could feel my face burning. She saw my predicament, which made her smile even more.

She patted my hand.

"It's all right; I'm ninety-one years old and proud of it. I've watched my husband die and I've watched my children die. No loving God would ever do that to a person."

I wondered what great sin she had perpetrated to incur so much of God's wrath. What could I say to a person who has gone through so much grief and still seems to have all the answers? I just lowered my eyes out of total respect for this amazing woman.

"People never really leave you, you know," she continued. "Everyone you love leaves a little bit of goodness within you, and it is this goodness that can be passed on to other people time and time again throughout the ages. I still ask Bert his opinion, even though I know the answer. That part of himself that he shared with me allows me to see problems from a different perspective, with some surprising conclusions. Of course, we all expect this to live on in our children after we die. In my case that can't happen, so I try to help other people in the hope that I will gain some small part of immortality through their future actions. What is life about if not to help others?"

I was stunned! Nothing I could add to the conversation would match the profundity of her deliberations on life. Yet through all the pain and suffering she had endured throughout the years, this was no dialectic theory. She was living her beliefs without any apparent need for the assent of her peers; without thousands of years of religion clouding the issue. She was certain of her beliefs and I am sure nothing could have shaken them. I made a silent vow to myself then and there that if I ever got to be that age, I would be just as certain of my beliefs.

There was a nudge on my arm and a frail hand offered me the inevitable breadcrumbs.

"Would you like to help me feed them?" she asked.

The deep conversation was over and two generations of relative strangers from completely different backgrounds, sat there on the park bench feeding the birds.

As I was helping her up to leave, I wondered how such strength could possibly come from such a frail body.

I watched her slowly move down the path until she was out of sight, before I returned to the diary.

# CHAPTER 17

Fr. Ryan did not go straight home. Instead, he went to the centre, apologising to Mrs. Bryant for his lateness and making some excuse about some people needing his help. One of the good things about being in his position was that he was not questioned on his work (at least not by his parishioners). The people knew that he was, by nature of his work, privy to many secrets and that part of his life had to be kept covert. With this trust came the burden of honesty, but his excuse was genuine. If the disk did prove that there were God's creatures on this earth who were not granted the right to a Christian teaching, they certainly did need his help.

He stayed at the centre for a few hours, always expecting Spider or the police to turn up, but the time passed without event.

It was evening before Fr. Ryan finally plucked up the courage to boot up his computer. He hoped it would work, as he had not shut it down properly. Feeling safe at not having to go online, he relaxed a little but he did need to delete the pornography files. He breathed a sigh of relief as the computer booted up as usual. He could hardly take it for repair if it had not!

Feeling better once the files were no longer on his computer, he inserted the disk with a certain amount of excitement and opened it full page, making notes in his diary, some in the form of questions to ask the man in the confessional, whom he was sure he would speak to again.

It took me a long time to decipher these notes but I eventually managed to piece them together and what I read shocked me as much as it must have shocked the priest.

It began with a report on the interrogation of the captured alien at Roswell in July 1947. The alien was injured and the medical aid available was not sufficient to restore him to health. In late July of that year, contact was made with the rest of the alien race, who wanted their injured colleague returned for treatment. The report recommended that it would be more beneficial to the technology of mankind to have the aliens treat him on Earth.

The reply to this report indicated that this was not the first contact with the aliens. It stated that mankind had not passed the first two safety tests for gaining entry to the G.F.

This was ringed by the priest with a big question mark over it.

The report continued with a request by the aliens for a progress report on mankind's development over the last four thousand years.

Another ring and two question marks surrounded this passage. The American government appeared to be willing to trade a life to gain technology from a race whose development far exceeded ours! But what was this progress report all about?

Internal correspondence then followed in earnest between various governmental departments. Some departments suggested returning the alien to show good faith to this peaceful race in the hope that they would change their minds about sharing their technology. Other departments suggested that more could be gained by interrogating the captive alien and the parts of his craft that had survived. This department claimed that it had already gained a wealth of technological information and suggested that to return the captive would show a weakness in mankind, which could be very dangerous in the light of their considerably advanced technology. The war department finally won the day in the 'interests of global security'. It was decided that a report should be drafted claiming that the alien had died, despite mankind's best efforts to save his life. The body, along with the bodies of the dead aliens were to have been destroyed in a terrible accident, a fire perhaps. The alien at this time was apparently recovering from his injuries and his knowledge would prove invaluable to the military in the event of an attack from other worlds.

'THIS IS NOT RIGHT!' the priest wrote in large capitals. There is a whole race out there, which has never heard of God!

Fr. Ryan felt a great weight lift from his shoulders at the realisation of his true vocation. God had sent him a messenger in the form of the man in the confessional. So what if he thought that Jesus was an extra-terrestrial? Christ did not originate on the earth so in a way he was extra-terrestrial! The rest was just semantics. The priest felt sure that he could convince the man that Jesus was the Son of God and work with him to spread this word beyond the mere boundaries of the earth.

"Thank you Jesus," he said with his eyes lifted up to heaven. "I know that with your help I can spread your word throughout all of your heavenly creations."

A final report stated that the aliens were taking the case to the. G.C. This seemed to panic the government and frantic reports were tossed around between various military and governmental departments recommending that all future military strategies must be aimed at protecting the Earth from an alien attack. Thus was the concept of the Star Wars Project born.

Fr. Ryan began to write a plan of attack. Firstly, he would have to get the bishop on his side so he would make a copy of the disk for him. He had already compiled a list of questions for the man in the confessional who would now have to come out and make himself known, to add credibility to the argument. Once the full weight of the church was behind him, the government would have to admit their covert operations and leave the way open for mankind to have contact with this seemingly harmless race. Only the church as an international organisation had the power to do this.

Fr. Ryan was excited by this prospect and momentarily allowed the childish notion of his being a secret agent, flit through his mind.

He checked the road outside for signs of people watching him, careful not to move the curtain. The road was empty. He wondered what would happen if people came to arrest him, and he looked for a place to hide the disk. After glancing round the room briefly, he walked through the door that led into the church and headed for the sacristy, pausing briefly to genuflect in front of the alter. He remembered a ciborium that had a loose base and wondered if the disk would fit inside. He opened the cupboard and took the cup from its velvet cover. He never used this ciborium because he was afraid that the very bottom of the base might fall off, but now he was struggling to pull it off. With a little more effort and a twist of the wrist, the base finally came free and the priest was delighted that the disk fitted snugly inside. He looked around him, even though he knew he was alone, at least from any earthly presence. Replacing the ciborium, complete with disk, he entered the main part of the church again and knelt down to pray.

He loved the peace and tranquillity of an empty church. His silent prayers echoed from the walls and the answers came back with equal volume. He prayed for the strength and wisdom to perform the great task that he would face, and for the minor miracle of mellowing the bishop's attitude towards him. He sat back on a pew. The sweet smell of incense still hung faintly in the air and the memories of past services were recorded in the very walls themselves. Here was a place of peace, a place where he could really talk to God. From the alter came the source of all knowledge, channelled by the statue of the Sacred Heart on one side and the Blessed Virgin on the other. From the crucifix hanging behind the alter came a new life from the blood of the one who made the ultimate sacrifice for mankind. The statues seemed to be looking on him with loving eyes and it was then that he knew that God would help him in his quest. If he had been chosen by the almighty, nothing could stand in his way, not even the bishop!

Even reading about the priest's unquestioning faith did not encourage me to attend church again with my family. I was a social leper to the people there. These were people who had the money and the time that allowed them to be able to indulge in the luxury of the faith that bound them together into their exclusive group. What did they know of the rigours of life, of the struggle to find work and hold a family together? They had their God who sorted out everything for them.

I longed to be able to feel what the priest felt in his empty church, but now I had been so abandoned by God that I could no longer bear even to think about him. So I returned to the routine of dropping-off my family at church and retiring to the park to read the diary if it was sunny, or returning home to read it if it was wet.

# CHAPTER 18

The sky looked angry and the wind was starting to pick up as I entered through the park gates. I had almost decided to go home instead, but thought that the rain might hold off for another hour or so.

A lone figure sat on the park bench, the collar on her thick plaid coat turned up high. A small pile of leaves was beginning to gather around her feet and the sparrows she was feeding had their feathers momentarily restyled by the gusts of wind.

This time it was my turn to ask if I could join her. It was a rhetorical question as the smile was there as ever and I was offered the inevitable handful of breadcrumbs.

I sat there for a few minutes in quiet contemplation, watching the steady stream of breadcrumbs slip through my fingers, taken by an invisible force in the direction of the waiting birds.

"You seem troubled," she eventually said, breaking the spell I was under.

"I can't find work."

She patted the back of my hand.

"You know every situation in life is both good and bad. Being out of work is bad for the finances, but it does give you more time to spend with your family."

"Yes, there is that," I sighed.

"Yet you sit here in the park? Don't you want to be with them?"

"I'm only in the way at home."

"Ah, you've had words."

I have always thought this phrase to be one of the more unusual that the English language has to offer. Words were surely not bad, yet to have them most certainly was!

"The greatest barrier to world harmony is a misunderstanding of what the other person is thinking. When we meet somebody for the first time, we build up a story around them.

Our minds will not accept a lack of knowledge so it fills in the gaps. All reactions towards that person are propounded by a story we've invented. Even when we know a person well, especially if we love them, a new story can develop around our personal doubts and insecurities. Things people say can be interpreted in a multitude of ways and picking the worst scenario is not always the wisest choice. Do you think that your wife wants to hurt you?"

Her logic was impeccable and yet she had built up a story about me. She was not there at the time! I decided to fill in a few gaps.

"I went to church the other day."

"And did you enjoy it."

"No, I only went because my wife goes every week. I thought it might bring us closer together."

This time she gave my hand a squeeze.

"She married you for what you are. Do you think it would please her if you changed into somebody else? I told you before that I thought you were a good man, and you've told me nothing that would change that opinion. Do you object to your wife going to church?"

"Not at all, she's always done it."

"And has she ever objected to your not going?"

"No, never."

"Then why change anything?"

The pat on my hand ensured me that she knew I did not have an answer to this.

"Deep inside you, you know what is right. Don't ever let anybody sway you from this knowledge. Your wife is your lifelong partner, not a rival to be vied with for position or status."

This old lady still amazed me. She really did believe that life was simple and I felt that she was probably right. A journey usually goes better if it is planned well from the beginning. My journey through life had already begun and getting back on the right track would take a lot more strength and knowledge than I felt I possessed at that time. I was comforted by the fact that the woman was convinced that I would make it.

The wind had all but disappeared by the time she took her leave and I sat there thinking about what she had said. Perhaps I had misinterpreted some of the things that Alison had said, but Nigel was certainly not a figment of my imagination. However, Nigel was not the problem. If Alison wanted somebody else, it must be because she was fed-up with me! I tried to look at things from her point of view. She had a husband who loved her and provided for his family. Now he cannot find work and therefore can no longer be a provider. This broke down to it all being my fault. From my point of view, I am trying my hardest to find work, but she does not seem to realise this. She told me that we were just getting by! Before this year, she had always been able to rely on my income, yet recently I had lost two jobs in quick succession. My fault again! The woman was right, it did all break down to a lack of understanding, but I knew how hard I had been trying. The lack of understanding was all on Alison's side!

I decided that I could at least prevent any further arguments by not responding to them.

I picked up the diary and walked briskly to the church car park. I would wait in the car. That way I would avoid meeting Nigel and pre-empt any arguments.

The next few days saw an uneasy tension at home, marked with forced politeness and extra attention paid to each other. It was a surreal state to be in, each seemingly willing the other to break and slip back into the normal friendly lifestyle we both so desperately wanted. We had become relative strangers overnight and even the children seemed to be joining in. True, there were no arguments but this was not the relationship that any of us wanted. We were at an impasse in our lives and I could see no way out. God had abandoned me, my family was in the process of doing so and the old lady in the park had told me that life was simple. How can it be simple if you do not know which way to turn? Perhaps she was wrong! I do not know why but I felt immensely guilty that that thought had ever entered my mind.

Unresolved problems need careful consideration but I, like many other people, favoured escapism. So I found myself sitting in the park once again with the diary, climbing into someone else's world.

# CHAPTER 19

Fr. Ryan sat in the confessional and yawned. Sometimes confessional sessions seemed to go on forever and he longed for the quiet solitude of an empty church. He also hoped that the man would come to speak to him again, not only for the stimulating level of conversation, but also because he wanted certain questions answered. He had his notes with him but it had been a few minutes since the last penitent had received forgiveness and a quick peek through the latticed door showed him that the church was empty. He should wait until eight o'clock when confession time was officially over, but was severely tempted to slope-off early. His water bottle was almost empty and the stuffiness of the confessional told him that his deodorant was beginning to fail. Five minutes to go. He swigged at the last of his water, just as he heard the click of the confessional door opening.

"Bless me father, for I have sinned."

It was him! The priest got excited as he fumbled for his notes in the dim light.

"You have some questions for me?" said the haunting voice through the grill.

"Indeed I do," replied the priest as he strained his eyes to read his notes. "First of all, why did you try to warn me off talking to the gangs?"

"It was a test, father. One which you passed admirably. If you had heeded my warnings, you wouldn't be of any use to me."

"Use? What, as regards having this alien released and contacting other alien races? Why me? I'm only a priest. You could have sent this information to the cardinals, or even the pope."

"All will become clear, but let us just say for the moment that the higher up one goes in any organisation, the more possibility there is of corruption. While I don't know if the Vatican is corrupt, I do know that you're not and I trust your judgement on the matter."

This seemed slightly patronising but it still encouraged the priest to warm to this man. He read the next question on his notes.

"What does M.I.R. stand for?"

"It stands for the modification of ideology in religion. It's an international committee that decides the modern doctrines of religions. It sorts out problems like the Banco Ambrosiano crash caused by covert dealings with the mafia and other bodies."

"I remember that," said the priest. "The Vatican was exonerated of all culpability in the matter. It only dealt with the bank in the same way as other states did, as a clearing bank."

"And as a gesture of goodwill, it gave the bank tens of m llions of pounds, putting the Vatican into the red for the first time in history. It's a pity that it didn't show the same goodwill towards the Italian earthquake victims!"

"Well if anybody had information of malpractice, wouldn t this have been brought to light at the time?"

"Roberto Calvi did, but in a fit of remorse he put a brick in his pocket, tied his hands behind his back and hanged himself from Blackfriars Bridge. But more on M.I.R. later.

"But there was an enquiry by the Vatican."

"Indeed there was, but with at least one of the four people involved being a pro-Nazi banker, the result was always going to be a foregone conclusion. Before we go any further I need to know if you have what it takes to pass the next test."

"The next test? What do I need to do for this one?"

"You need to be able to listen with an open mind to what I'm about to tell you, regardless of your past or current beliefs on the subject. I can provide evidence for most of it and the gaps can be filled by deduction. Are you happy to at least try this? I will endeavour to answer any questions you might have."

Fr. Ryan would have agreed to listen to practically anything if it led to the knowledge of an alien race. The fact that this man thought that one of these creatures was God, did not matter in the slightest.

"I'll listen to anything you have to say."

"Good, then let's start at the beginning. Do you believe in Adam and Eve and the garden of Eden?"

Fr. Ryan could not see the connection with aliens and he thought for a moment before answering. He had heard people ask that if Adam and Eve had Cain and Abel, where did their wives come from? There were various answers to this question but personally, the priest thought of this section of Genesis as being purely parabolic.

"I believe in original sin," he said cautiously. "But the idea of two people living in a garden is purely symbolic."

"I believe that there were two people but that the forbidden fruit was not an apple, but a union with man. Was it not woman who tempted man?"

Fr. Ryan knew all about the race of giants, first mentioned in the book of Genesis. He had many discussions about the subject while he was at university. This race, called the Nephilim were assumed to be foreign settlers and held in awe because of their advanced culture, rather than their being from another planet.

"These aliens bred with mankind but their offspring took on more of man's traits of greed and violence towards each other and the council decided that it wasn't working."

"The council?"

"Yes, the Galactic Council (G.C.). They make all the decisions for the Galactic Federation (G.F.). What I told you about a confederation of peaceful planets was absolutely true. I don't expect you to believe me at this point, but bear with me. As I said, I have proof for most of what I'm telling you. The council decided that it could not let a violent, warring planet survive to create problems for the federation in the future. And so it was decided to destroy the Earth. It was only an intervention at the eleventh hour by one called Noah that convinced the council to reprieve the Earth. He convinced them that by drastically culling the Earth's population, more of the Nephilim traits would show through. And so the great flood was formed."

The priest thought he should say something at this point, if only to defend his faith.

"If these were aliens, who made them?"

"Perhaps God made them, I don't know."

This was not the answer he was expecting, but now he was getting into this man's theory and wanted to know more.

"Why was it such a great sin to mate with the people of Earth?"

"The Nephilim are not a race in themselves, rather a section of philosophers, the watchers, only there to observe and make reports on mankind's progress. When the council found out what had been going on, they were convinced to wait and see what the outcome would be. You see this race doesn't normally mate until they're a few hundred of our Earth years old. Noah was five hundred when he had his first son and his father lived to be seven hundred and seventy. Had Noah not convinced the council, we wouldn't be having this conversation now."

Fr. Ryan was trying to find the weaknesses in the man's argument.

"With all these visits from outer space, surely someone would have seen a spacecraft at one time or another."

"Indeed. Most of the landings would have been in remote areas such as in the desert or near the top of a mountain, but there was one well documented landing a few thousand years ago. A saucer-shaped craft came down and hovered above the ground. Four creatures in space suits got out and walked along with the craft on umbilicals. Their faces could not be seen because of their tinted visors, but the emblems of the federation could be clearly seen on either side of their helmets: the lion for courage and the ox for strength, topped by the eagle, as a symbol of their spacecraft if you like. People think of alien worlds as being vastly different from our own, but what the natural world chooses as viable under one set of climatic conditions would be likely to be similar under the same set of conditions elsewhere."

"I'm sorry, but you can't possibly know with any certainty what landed on Earth thousands of years ago, let alone what insignia it had. You said it was documented. Where?"

"In Ezekiel, chapter one, verse fifteen, I believe.

The man's voice never changed its calm, haunting tone. He seemed to have all the information at his fingertips. Fr. Ryan felt that he was down a number of points in this discussion so he decided to question the man rather than let him wax-lyrical.

"So where does all the information about this so called federation come from, or is it all just theory?"

"Whether or not you believe that the Old Testament in an accurate portrayal of ancient history is something you must decide for yourself, but information about the federation is far more current and well documented, but we'll come to that part. Just to recap, we have a confederation of planets that have evolved by working together for the common good. They are looking to increase their membership but they can't afford to include races that can't live in peace, even on their own planet. They send down some observers, early in man's development. These observers began to integrate with the people of Earth, but mankind's development is not conducive to peace. Since man's technology would develop in time, it was decided that it was better to destroy the Earth, than to risk future conflict. Noah, a much respected descendent of their race, appealed to the council claiming that it was against the constitution of the confederation to destroy a race without first trying to influence its development. It was a close call, but the council finally decided that a radical culling of the population was necessary in order to be able to influence those remaining. And so they culled the people by flood. The council also reserved the right to insert teachers, prophets to guide man on the right path towards peace."

Fr. Ryan was feeling a little uneasy at the way this conversation was going. He was starting to sweat and the little wooden room was closing in around him. He was fascinated by the conversation but he would much prefer it to be held in a more relaxed place.

"Shall we continue this conversation in my living room? We'll have to meet face to face at some point if we're to show a united front for the release of this alien."

"It's better that we don't meet unless it's absolutely necessary. There's a bottle of water just outside your door if you're thirsty."

The priest opened the door slightly and picked up the bottle from the ground. The cool air swirled around the little room and the light made him squint. He began to close the door but the church was now empty and the cool air too inviting, so he left it ajar.

"Don't worry father, it's no miracle, just forward thinking on my part."

This was the first hint at humour the man had ventured and it made the priest feel a little more relaxed. He wanted to keep the man's theories on a more light-hearted vein. He had said that he would listen to what he had to say, but he did not have to agree with it.

"I suppose you're going to tell me that Jesus Christ was an alien."

"Father, I would not presume to attempt to call your beliefs into question. Belief that Christ was the son of God is irrelevant to the point I'm trying to get across."

Fr. Ryan did not think it was irrelevant. This was the point that he was trying to get across to the man. The Old Testament was fraught with anomalies, but the life of Christ was something that he understood very well.

"But you indicated that you thought he was an alien, from reading about his life. What evidence do you have for this?"

The man sighed. He obviously did believe this to be irrelevant, but the priest saw this as an inroad into converting this man to the true faith. Without this belief, why would he be so concerned about one alien who was allegedly held captive?

"Very well father. I really didn't want to get into this and at the end of the day it all breaks down to what you want to believe. I don't want us to argue on this point.

Mary was impregnated by, can we agree to call it a non-Earth life form? Next came the magi, led by a star, which shone on the stable where the infant was born. I'm sure they were led there, but I'm equally certain it was not by a star. How could a star lead them, let alone shine in just one place?

Since his life was based on peace and love, Christ couldn't resist helping people with the medical science that was beyond man's ability at that time."

"Did that include raising people from the dead?" interjected the priest.

"The Celtic origin of having a wake was to leave the body for a certain period of time to make sure that the person was in fact dead. There is much evidence of people being accidentally buried alive. It would have been no different in those days."

"And what about Christ's passion, ending with him dying on the cross? Would an alien have gone through all of that for a race that might have to be destroyed anyway?"

"That was never supposed to have happened. He was dying anyway and was supposed to have 'died' in custody."

"Why do you think he was dying?" Fr. Ryan was quite amused by the man's theory, but also quite surprised that he seemed to have all parts of it covered. He still could not understand why the man wanted to bring him through the history of mankind, simply to release an alien, but the conversation was far more stimulating than he usually got in the confessional so he continued to listen as he had promised.

"He sweated blood in Gethsemane. Any medic will tell you that this is a sure sign of the body breaking down. Any person who lived the life that he did and preached as he did in an occupied country, would have known that he would have been arrested and executed. Yet he showed no apparent fear of this forthcoming event until news that technicalities prevented his being spirited away after his apparent death in custody and that he would have to go through the actual execution. This terrified him, as it would anybody. Fortunately, they did manage to send down an.......angel with a powerful drug, which would take away most of the pain. Unfortunately, this meant that he couldn't speak at his trial or carry his cross very far, but it was all they could manage at short notice."

"And the resurrection?"

"Yes, they only just managed that. Do you remember when Mary entered the tomb and saw two angels? They had been working on Christ to get him in a stable condition to be able to move him. He had only just been moved when Mary entered and a hologramic image of him was sent down to fulfil the prophesy of the resurrection. That's why Mary wasn't allowed to touch him. There was nothing there to touch!"

"So you don't believe in heaven and hell?"

"Certainly I do, but let me first say that every living thing dies, even aliens, although they do have a longer life span than we do. Thirty seconds is not a long time, but you try holding your hand in a candle flame for that long. Time is relative and everything we experience is done so retrospectively. If you go to sleep with problems on your mind or an intense disliking for someone, you have a restless night's sleep because these feelings are bad for the body and produce toxins. Conversely, when everything is peaceful in your life, you sleep well and have happy dreams. Death is similar to sleep except that you never wake up. Since all experiences are retrospective, it's impossible to experience the end of your life and the good or bad feelings you do experience constitute your eternity. Therefore, you create your own heaven or hell by the way you live your life and to you, this will last for eternity even though others may watch you die.

Fr. Ryan decided to call a halt to this onslaught on his religious beliefs.

"You surely don't expect me to believe this ridiculous, simplified version of our saviour's life? He said.

"No, of course not," was the unexpected reply. "More importantly, I don't want us to fall out over it. A person's beliefs are his own and I respect your faith. I only ask that you afford me the same courtesy."

Fr. Ryan could not argue with his point of view, but he longed for the opportunity discuss this matter further. Perhaps the opportunity would present itself at a later date. For now, he wanted to learn more about the captured alien.

"What does all this have to do with M.I.R?" He asked.

"Christians believe that everybody is equal. It's basically a left-wing organisation."

"Hold on a minute," said the priest, thinking that this was developing into a political discussion. "The Christian religion is apolitical!"

"Hmm," said the man. He seemed to be getting annoyed at himself for not being able to find the correct words and phrases to make his point without causing offence. The priest appreciated his efforts but wished that he would come to the point. He obviously believed that he had something very important to say, but was nevertheless extremely cautious in the way he was saying it.

"Just tell it as you see it," said Fr. Ryan in an effort to speed-up the conversation. "I'm not easily shocked, or convinced."

"Thank you," replied the man in a very genuine manner, which showed that he was not in the least phased by the priest's last comment. "The theories of communism or socialism are loosely based on equality for all, although man's versions of them don't seem to work quite as well as they should. Nevertheless, they are much closer to the teachings of the various religious factions throughout the world than their rival, capitalism. M.I.R. was initiated to keep religion as far right-wing as possible."

"That doesn't make sense," said the priest. "Why would they want to do that?"

"To people in power, the concept of everybody being equal is unconscionable! They had, and indeed still have to keep it right wing in order to hang on to that power. That is why the very word 'communist' is treated as an insult in many developed countries and wars have been fought to keep it at bay."

"You mean like the Vietnam war?" said the priest in an effort to show that he was keeping up with the conversation. "But the Second World War was a fight against the extremely right-wing Nazi movement."

"The Second World War was a struggle between the Nazi right-wing and the Russian left wing, but American and European involvement in it was simply a right-wing power struggle."

"But the people of this country, as well as our allies, were fighting to destroy Nazism! If not, what were the Nuremberg trials all about?"

"Nuremberg was a farce. Most of the important Nazi's were helped to escape and given new identities in Europe and Latin

America. This was all organised by M.I.R. as was the kidnap and subsequent assassination of the socialist leader Aldo Moro and the assassination of Pope John Paul 1."

Fr. Ryan was astounded by this last comment.

"Why would they have killed the pope? He was loved by everybody!"

"His father once stood for election as a socialist candidate and he himself was known to favour socialism. He would have sacked the American head of the Vatican bank and opened-up a whole can of worms."

"In what way? Surely the Vatican is allowed to have a bank."

"Of course it is, but the fact that the Vatican bank funded the escape of Nazi war criminals might not have been fully understood by the good Christian people. Neither would some of the darker dealings instigated by the bishop in charge of it. And so M.I.R. decided that the Pope should have a heart attack. They were careful to cover their tracks by not having an autopsy and by having the body embalmed very quickly, but not as careful at instructing the staff about the cover story."

"But wasn't there a danger that the incoming pope might have done the same thing, or do you think that his election was also part of a massive conspiracy?"

"Judge for yourself. A left-wing pope in fine health with the best of medical care dies thirty-three days after taking office. A polish right-wing pope who sanctioned the channelling of vast amounts of Vatican funds to the polish shipyard workers, thereby smashing the communists hold over the country, survives an assassination attempt."

"That's simply conjecture," said the priest. "You can't prove any of it."

"You're right, I can't prove that there was a conspiracy, but most of what I have told you is verifiable. Most of what you preach is not verifiable and needs an enormous degree of faith, even to accept the basic logic of it."

The man seemed to be getting agitated because Fr. Ryan was not convinced, and this showed in his voice. Realising this he quickly tried to remedy the situation.

"I'm sorry father, I shouldn't have said that. As I've already told you, your faith is your own and not in the least bit relevant to what I have to tell you."

Fr. Ryan's patience was wearing thin. The man had given him lots of unsubstantiated theories about religion and the Bible, but he wanted to know about this captured alien. At one point, he thought that the man was trying to convert him to atheism, but now he was not certain what his point was.

"I've listened carefully to all your theories but I still don't understand where you're going with all of this," he said.

"I do appreciate your patience father and now I will explain. After Roswell, the Americans panicked. They felt certain that the Galactic council would condemn the Earth to obliteration and so they set about preparing for an attack from outer space. It was even called the Star Wars Project! Haven't you ever wondered why a so called civilised Earth would want the means to obliterate itself many times over?"

"Well yes, but wasn't there a movement towards unilateral disarmament?"

"Yes, but only after the judgement of the council was announced."

"And what was that judgement?"

"The judgement was a reversible destruction of the Earth."

"Reversible?"

"By shifting the jet stream and increasing global warming, it was thought that mankind would have to forget their differences and use technology to work together in a common cause. This obviously isn't working and man is going to wipe himself out through his own greed. The information I asked you to look at confirms this but our best hope is to get the government to release the alien so that he can confirm this himself. People are not easily convinced by official documents, and it would take a powerful lobby to get him released, but I believe it can be done. That's where you and others like you come in."

The priest felt a little deflated that he was not the only one who had been chosen to be privy to this information, but also relieved that he was not being asked to shoulder this burden of knowledge alone. He repeated the question he had asked before.

"Why me?"

"Everybody was chosen for the unique contacts they have. Whatever reason compels you to accept this challenge, you are the only one of the group in your particular position. Now I have to ask you, are you prepared to help?"

Fr. Ryan thought for a moment before he spoke. The parts of the document he had read confirmed much of what the man had said and he was sure that a closer inspection of them would confirm the decision of the galactic council, but not of course the man's views of God!"

"I'm not in the least convinced about your interpretation of the bible and I certainly don't agree with your atheistic views, but the documents I've read so far have convinced me that there is a captured alien life form on Earth and the only reason I would agree to help would be to spread the word of Jesus to another race of God's creatures. If you're prepared to accept that, then I'm prepared to help. What would I have to do?"

"I'm very glad to have you on board father and as I have said, your religious beliefs don't affect the cause. You might be interested to know that there are many faiths, as well as atheists and agnostics involved. This really is all about forgetting our differences and working together for the good of mankind. Spread the word through as many channels as you can, but be careful. Tell only those people you can trust. As you can imagine, there are many powerful people like Opus Dei who stand to lose a lot through exposure. When we have enough people, our efforts will be coordinated and the governments will have to concede. I must go now. You've got all the information you'll need. Study it carefully."

"How will I contact you?"

"You can't. I have a lot of work to do, but at the crucial time I'll be there."

"Just one more question before you go. You told me when we first spoke that you were going to kill someone. Was that just to get my attention?"

"It might still happen, but I hope not. I have never killed anyone but if the event does arrive, I hope I'll have the strength to carry it out."

"I'll pray for you," said the priest as he watched through the half-open door as the figure left through the church.

# CHAPTER 20

I closed the diary and rubbed my eyes. The bright sun reflecting from the pages had made them sore and I had to blink several times to be able to focus on the park. It was a feeling I had experienced before when I had been deeply engrossed in a novel. The book had been my reality for so long, that when I put it down, my surroundings seemed unreal and a certain silence ensued as if the book had been reading aloud to me.

A small plastic bag dropped into my lap. The woman was breathless as she slumped down beside me.

"Can you open that for me?" she gasped. "The knot's a bit tight for my fingers."

I easily untied the knot and handed her the bag of breadcrumbs.

"And how has your life been since we last spoke?"

"Still no work," I replied wistfully.

"No your real life!"

The question confused me. Did she not consider work to be part of real life?

"In a couple of years you won't even remember being out of work, but you'll always remember the arguments."

"I just can't seem to win, whatever I do."

"Of course not. I can't understand why you keep trying."

Now I really did not know what she was talking about. She did not consider work to be real life and now she seemed to think that I should simply agree with everything Alison said to me! Perhaps the old lady was not as wise as I first took her to be. Once again, she seemed to read my thoughts and patted the back of my hand in comfort.

"Let me explain. If you were working for a company and a better job became available with more money and better conditions, would you take the new job?"

181

"Yes, of course."

"Why?"

"To earn more money and have a better lifestyle, of course."

"And then if you were given one million pounds, would you continue to work?"

"Well no, I wouldn't need to."

"So work is just a means to an end."

"Yes of course, but it's important. It's my job to earn money to look after my family."

The woman was still breathless as she paused for thought.

"And what is your wife's job?"

"Well, she looks after the house and family while I'm out at work."

"So presumably, if she was given one million pounds, she wouldn't need you anymore."

"No, you don't understand," I said in panic at the woman's apparent attack on my family. "It's not all about money. My wife loves me and I love her. We're a family unit."

"Well, if you are living as one, is arguing with her any different from arguing with yourself? It doesn't matter who wins, you both lose because you are one. If you argue with one of your friends, about football for instance, and you prove your point and win the argument, it makes you feel good. How good does it make you feel to win an argument against your wife?"

I had to admit that it never made me feel good to argue with Alison.

"Real life is all about people and how you interact with them, not how much money you have or how you can brow-beat people into submission. I can see that you love your wife very much. If you buy her a bunch of flowers, it makes you happy because she's happy. When she's ill, it makes you feel sad because she's in pain, not because she can't perform her job as efficiently. When you are out of work it makes your wife sad because you are sad, not because you're not performing your job as efficiently."

She gave me a moment to reflect on the things she had said. She was right of course and I now thought that perhaps I was beginning to understand her views on life. Then I thought of Nigel and all the friends my wife had at church. This was a life that she led away from me; one from which I seemed to be excluded. I tried to show willing by going with her, but that was a disaster. Perhaps the old lady had an answer to this.

"Can two people really be a couple if part of their lives is led separately and in secret?"

"Certainly."

She paused briefly to collect her thoughts.

"You told me you played rugby, pitting your skill and strength against other big men."

"Yes, but rugby is only a game."

"Agreed, but do you play with your children in the same competitive way and sing rude songs with them afterwards?"

I was not aware that old ladies knew what went on in a rugby club bath and I felt a little uneasy that she possessed such knowledge.

"Of course you don't. That is a separate part of your life, one in which your attitude changes completely. It doesn't make the slightest difference to your family whether or not you score a try. They're not playing the game but they're happy because you're happy. Your achievement is their achievement, your pride their pride. If not, why would you bother to mention it to them?"

Again she was right but it did not address the point I was trying to make.

"Alison goes to church every Sunday. That's an exclusive community that looks down on people like me."

"A group of people huddled together in a room for moral support, waiting for someone to stand in front of them and tell them how they should live their lives, does not have the right to look down on anybody! Why do you find them a threat?"

"They talk about loving God more than anyone else."

"And you're frightened that Alison loves God more than she loves you? Why not ask her? If she really believes, she will have an answer, if not then the threat is eliminated."

She patted my hand and I knew the sermon was coming to an end.

"Always remember," she concluded. "Everybody you meet has the same doubts and uncertainties in life that you have. There are many right ways to live life and just because a person's ideas are different from yours, it doesn't make either of you wrong. Always look for the good in any person or situation you come across. Pick a notorious figure from history, if you like, and try to say something good about him."

I immediately thought of Adolph Hitler and could think of nothing good to say about him, but perhaps this was an unfair example and I took the lady's point.

"I'm sure there's enough love left over from your family life to share with others. Always put the things that are important to you first and share your happiness with everybody you meet. That way a small part of you will live on in others and the world will become a better place."

She offered me a handful of breadcrumbs and I knew she had finished talking. The conversation had obviously worn her out and we both sat there feeding the sparrows.

A blackbird sang in a nearby tree, such a beautiful, piercing sound that my whole reality seemed to balance on the tip of every note. I wondered what unimaginative soul named the composer of this wonderful melody. Life must be so simple to a blackbird. He has no home, he has to hunt for food every day or he will starve, the snows of winter might kill him and yet he sings his way through life with all the strength in his tiny body.

My mind was cast back to a passage from the Bible I had heard as a child: 'look at the birds of the air, they neither reap nor sow.......' I had never understood that passage. Did it mean that one did not have to bother working? This seemed unlikely. I thought about the diary and wondered why the aliens might have used those words. They might have come down to earth and heard the birds singing about what a wonderful thing it is simply to be alive! After meeting man, they might have also wished that it was the birds that they were sent here to watch.

The bird poured out another beautiful melody, quickly joined by a flock of smaller birds that chirruped energetically, all agreeing how good life was. The sounds dissolved my problems into insignificance. Where were their cars? Where were their detached houses and their big bank accounts? Where was their God? They really knew what life was all about. I had far more than they had, yet I was not as happy! Life was far more complex in the world of man, but why? What did they have that I did not? I reversed the question in my mind. The things that I had that they did not were of little importance. If Alison and I were both millionaires independently, would we then have more than we have now or less of the things that really mattered? I decided on less, as we would lose the satisfaction of the success we gained from working together. What then really mattered in my life? Proving that I was a good provider and a hard worker? The last people we should ever have to prove anything to are our loved ones.

I suddenly had an overwhelming urge to hold my family tightly in my arms. They were all that really mattered to me. What had I been doing to them? What was I trying to prove?

From reading the man's interpretation of the Bible and remembering the old lady's words, I realised that anything can be interpreted in a number of ways. Despite any evidence to the contrary, the priest was not convinced of the man's theories. Why? Was it because he judged all evidence from one basic assumption, that God created everything, and all other evidence was worked from this basic principle?

I also started from one basic principal. I loved my wife, and my children who were born from the union of that love. Perhaps I would have interpreted Alison's words and actions different y if I really loved her! What had happened to my basic theory? I DID love my wife! I knew that.

Panic began to take over. Why did I need to make such an affirmation?

My mind returned to the diary. The man did not seem to care whether there was a God. He was only interested in helping mankind. Conversely, the priest wanted to help mankind to learn about God. They both believed in the Bible, but the man's interpretation was not influenced by a belief in God. Which one was right? Perhaps they both were. Perhaps there is no ultimate right and the only wrong is in not following ones beliefs! Any being that came down from the sky in those days would have been interpreted as being a God. Indeed some national leaders have proclaimed themselves Gods.

Did I really believe in God? Looking at the evidence, I thought not. Why then did I feel guilty about not going to church? Probably because I was raised a catholic and the teachings one gets as a child have a deep-seated effect on the rest of that person's life.

My life was in tatters and I felt a strong urge to decide once and for all what I really believed. I was not a child anymore; I was a man and as such had to leave behind the teachings of my childhood. This was more difficult than I thought.

Something was wrong. There were no trumpets, no marching bands. The sun was still bright and the birds still sang sweetly, but I knew that an era had come to an end. I had to continue with my thoughts in this sacred place.

Where to begin? Whatever the purpose of the Bible, it was certainly a history book and I would think of it as such. So I decided to begin with God creating the heavens and the earth in seven days. This must be parabolic, as days were not invented when he began his creation. I would try to stick only to facts.

Pleased with this beginning, I thought of the next part of the Bible that I could remember. The Garden of Eden. This I decided was also a parable, as Cain and Abel would have had to have interbred with Eve, thereby depleting the gene pool and jeopardising man's survival, unless of course the man's theory was correct.

Genesis tells of a race of giants who mated with the people of the Earth. This race could not have come from the Garden of Eden; therefore, life did not begin by God creating only two people. I did not know the relevant passage in Ezekiel but I was, for the moment at least, prepared to accept that it did indeed describe the landing of a spacecraft.

The basic teachings of my childhood were slowly dissolving before my eyes and I felt a strange kind of cold isolation settle on my body like a gentle snowfall. God did not create the world in seven days. Mankind did not start in a garden with two people. If the world was created by an all-loving God, why did he say he was going to destroy it so early in man's development? I would have thought that he would have given his creation a little more time to prove itself. Man was no threat to God so time would have been immaterial to him. Furthermore, on reaching this omnipotent decision, how did one man manage to talk him out of it? Again, the man's theory seemed to hold more water.

I pulled my jacket tighter around my body, even though the sun was still shining.

I thought of my children kneeling in church and it angered me. I love my girls more than anything, but I would not want them to grovel at my feet, telling me how unworthy they were to be called my children! This is not the wish of a loving father, rather that of an egotistical despot! Certainly not one with whom I would want to spend eternity!

So, if there ever was a God, his existence is certainly not based on love.

Next, I turned my attention to the church. I remembered as a child being invited to kiss the bishop's ring. Kiss somebody's ring? Where did that fit in with Christ washing the feet of his disciples? People would crowd into the church when the bishop was there, just to get his blessing. I thought that blessings were supposed to come from God! The same applies in St. Peter's square when the Pope gives his blessing. The very title of 'Your Holiness' is indicative of a certain inequality in mankind.

I looked around me nervously, unsure if I had been speaking aloud. The passers-by did not give any indication that I had, so I returned to my thoughts.

Without having the facilities at hand to corroborate his evidence, I had to accept the man's version of the Vatican-funded ratlines to help Nazi war criminals escape. Equally, I had to accept that there was, at the very least, suspicion surrounding the death of Pope John Paul 1.

So it seemed that Christianity was run by a right-wing hierarchy, in total opposition to the teachings of Christ!

Where did that leave me? I was now convinced that there was no God. If I was wrong and he did exist, he would not be somebody I would like very much. If the teachings of Christ were the right path to take, then the church was the wrong way and vice versa.

I still had two burning questions that needed to be resolved. Firstly, if this information about the Bible and the political dealings of the church is so freely available, why do people still have an unquestioning faith in it? Was I missing the point somewhere along the line?

The second question was far more important to me. Did my wife love God more than she loved me? If I were able to ask her then and there, the answer would almost certainly have been a resounding yes.

Now I knew what was important in my life. I would not have swapped wealth or money for my family. Being with them was the only important thing in my life. I now understood what Alison had meant by getting by. We would get by as far as money was concerned while still enjoying the important part of our lives.

How could I have been so selfish? I had made my wife unhappy and my children were staying out of the way, simply because life was not going the way I wanted it to go. I had been worried about holding my family together whereas it was Alison who had been holding us all together.

The old lady was right. It was all based on a misunderstanding, but it was I who had misunderstood! I was feeling bad about being out of work and expectant of being shown the understanding that Alison already had. We were a unit and it took one old lady in a park to make me realise this.

I patted her hand.

"Your little bit of goodness will be passed on, you have earned your immortality," I said, though I knew she could not hear me.

I stood up and tucked in her collar. Looking into her face, I had a glimpse of paradise. She had won her heaven and somehow it seemed unkind to do anything to disturb it.

And so I just walked away from this lady who had added so much to my life. I do not believe that she would have wanted me to do anything more.

I hurried through the park, hoping it was not too late to put things right.

I was willing the bus to go faster, every stop taking an eternity. It was only when I got to the bottom of my road that my pace slowed. What was I going to say? I felt such remorse, yet I was afraid to face my own wife. I wondered what her reaction would be. Had I driven her into the arms of another man, Nigel the creep perhaps?

I took a deep breath before entering the house. There was silence. I stepped into the kitchen and saw a note lying on the table. I stepped out again, not wanting to read the content. Whatever happened now would be my fault, and I must handle it like a man. If Alison chose to leave me, I would have to accept her decision. But the girls! A moment of panic seized me. I could not live without my children!

My mind returned to the note on the table but I could not pluck up the courage to read it. The girls would not want to leave me, that decision would be made for them. I thought I had been trying my best but I now realise that I had been trying the wrong way. My family did not need a superman, they needed a father and I had failed them! Could they ever forgive me?

I had to read the note. I crept into the kitchen, trying to read it before it came fully into focus.

'We're at Nigel's,' it said.

Those first words hit me like a hammer. My whole body was trembling and I felt weak. I read on.

'His partner has been rushed to hospital and he needs someone to talk to. I've fed the girls and I'll cook us something when we get home around eight. Love, Ali.'

At least she was coming home and she did sign it: love Ali. Perhaps all was not lost.

I looked at my watch and noticed that my hands were still shaking. It was three o'clock. I had five hours to get myself together and decide what I was going to say. Perhaps I would cook her a meal. Yes, that would be a good idea.

I looked in the fridge and saw the fresh chicken. I checked the cupboard and found a packet of stuffing. Roast chicken, stuffing, roast potatoes and whatever vegetables I could find. I had often watched Alison cook a roast. I could do this!

The dinner did not need to go on for a few hours and I needed to keep my mind occupied to keep this sickly feeling in my stomach at bay, so I turned on the computer and put in a search.

I read about the Vatican-funded 'ratlines' which helped Nazi war criminals to escape, and about the nations which were complicit in these actions. I read about the Red and Black Brigades and the assassination of Aldo Moro, and of the secrecy surrounding the death of Pope John Paul 1.

I looked further and discovered the involvement of a very sinister group of ultra-wealthy right wing Catholics called Opus Dei and their alleged involvement in the death of Robert Calvi.

I put in a search for the Nephilim, not expecting to find anything and I was shocked to read that it was now generally assumed to be an alien race.

I went to the bedroom and found Alison's old family bible. Genesis was easy to find because I knew it was at the beginning, but Ezekiel took a little more searching for. It seemed strange to be reading a bible again and I still could not treat the book with anything but reverence.

Here, before my eyes, both in the Bible and on the web, was corroboration of what the man had told the priest. The Nephilim were never mentioned in any religious education that I ever had. Why not? Were Christians being treated like the African slaves were treated, being given enough religious instruction to enable them to live in a Christian society, but not enough to make them think they were equal, even in the sight of God? Was this why the Vatican consistently refused to release the rest of the Dead Sea Scrolls? Were the crusades the work of God or simply the product of bureaucratic empire building? Is it not equally wrong to kill innocent people in a terrorist attack, as it is to kill even more by bombing a country? Yet we are told that God is on our side and somehow, that makes everything all right!

This information is public knowledge, yet people still follow their religion! Surely even the most ardent believer must now realise that religion is being run for the sake of wealth and power, even if the original concept of it was true!

The man's explanation of the Bible and subsequent world events seemed far more plausible to me than the blind faith I was expected to have as a child, being raised in a catholic family.

I suddenly felt immensely powerful, not because I thought that I could change the world, but because the guilt that I had been carrying around with me all these years about being a lapsed catholic, had slipped from my shoulders. I was free to decide what I believed was important in my life. I loved my family far more than I could love any God, and I no longer felt guilty about saying so. Far from not being equal to the people who attended church, I now felt a little sorry for them. My life was real, while theirs was based on a little knowledge of unsound theories ventured by other people.

I must let Alison know about the things I have learned.

My stomach began to knot-up at the thought of facing my wife. Perhaps now was not the time. It could be the last straw if she thought I now wanted to take away her religion. I must be careful not to give her any excuse to leave. If she was happy in her beliefs, that is all that mattered. I just wanted her to give me the chance to prove that I was no longer feeling sorry for myself and that I could be a good husband and father.

I looked at my watch again. It was time to start preparing dinner. I walked to the kitchen, turned on the oven and began reading the instructions on the packet of stuffing.

'Empty contents into bowl and pour on boiling water'. That was simple enough. Encouraged by the results of my newfound cooking skills, I set about preparing the potatoes. Peeling them was not a problem and I chopped them and arranged them in the roasting tin around the freshly stuffed chicken. I looked at my watch again and realised that Alison would be home in an hour. I had to get a move on, so I turned up the oven to its maximum setting and put in the chicken at the very top. This was the hottest part of the oven and would cook the quickest. I chopped up the runner beans and put them in the saucepan.  They were nice, big beans, not the skinny things we usually have!  They would be delicious!

Next, I had to lay the table.  I found the lace tablecloth that Alison reserved for special occasions and some ornate candleholders that we were given as a wedding present.  Everything had to be perfect.

It was five minutes to eight and I turned on the vegetables.  I would not light the candles until she arrived.  I uncorked a bottle of white wine and carefully emptied out all the bits and pieces that were stored in the ice bucket.  There was no ice in the freezer so I half-filled the ice bucket with cold water from the tap and placed it in the centre of the table.  I polished the glasses as I surveyed my creation.  The scene was set, a veritable banquet for the lord and lady of the manor.

Five past eight, ten past.  I walked over to the window for the tenth time.  What if she did not come home?  I began to panic.

The chicken was a lovely light brown on top and I turned down the boiling beans.

I walked back to the window, just in time to see a black BMW pull up on the road outside. Nigel! Whatever happened, I would have to be pleasant to him. I would ask him about his partner, how long she is expected to be in hospital.

As I walked out the front door, even the sight of my wife kissing him on the cheek was not going to prevent me from being nice to him. This was my last chance and I would not blow it!

Nigel wound down the window and I smiled through gritted teeth as I approached the car.

"Thanks for lending me your wife for a few hours," he said.

His face was ashen.

"My pleasure," I said, still smiling. "How's your partner?"

"Ruptured appendix," was the grave reply. "But the doctors said he'll pull through all right. I got him to the hospital just in time."

Him! The look of relief must have shown in my face and was immediately interpreted as my having a lot of concern for my fellow man.

"Thanks for asking," he continued. "You've got a wonderful wife here. I don't know what I'd have done without her."

"Yes," I agreed. "I don't know what I'd do without her either. "Would you like to come in for a cuppa?" I asked, hoping he would decline.

"Thanks all the same but I'd better get home. It's nice to meet you again."

With that, Nigel drove away and I walked down the drive with Alison and two very sleepy little girls.

"That was good of you to ask about Nigel's other half. I know you don't really like him but you showed a lot of concern there. When it really matters, you always come up trumps. I'm very proud of you!"

This last comment was followed by a peck on the cheek and then a twitching of the nose as we entered the house.

"Have you left something on the cooker?" she asked, a sudden look of concern on her face.

"It's a surprise," I whispered.

"Well I think your surprise is burning," she whispered back mischievously.

Alison put the girls to bed as I rushed into the smoke-filled kitchen. I turned off everything and emptied the last drop of sizzling water through the colander. A bean flopped limply after it. I shook the saucepan and three more beans wrested their way from the bottom of the pan. Moving them around with a spoon, I noticed that it was only the black ones at the bottom that were really stuck. The rest could be rescued.

I took out the roast, just as I heard Alison coming down the stairs. Intercepting her in the hallway, I led her to the table and poured us both a glass of wine, dripping water over the tablecloth. This was not all going to plan!

"This is all very lovely," she said. "What's the occasion?"

I had rehearsed a speech in my mind many times during the last few hours. Now that the moment had arrived, my mind was blank.

"I just wanted to show you how much I love you," came from my lips, but it was not how the speech was supposed to have started.

Perhaps I should put my brain in neutral more often because this had the desired effect.

"Aww," she said as her gentle arms slid around my neck and pulled me close. "I love you too," she whispered in my ear.

I could have remained in that embrace forever but I eventually invited her to sit down, promising her a meal fit for a queen.

I returned to the kitchen and began to salvage the beans.

"Shall I light the candles?" she called.

I knew there was something I had forgotten to do!

"Yes please."

Picking up a pair of tongs, I carefully separated the limp green beans from the brittle black ones and placed a small portion on each plate. I put the plates on the table and returned to get the roast.

The top skin of the chicken was a little darker than I would have liked and I had to cut off the very black pieces, but I eventually arranged it on a carving dish with the potatoes I had prised from the bottom of the roasting pan, around it. Picking up my carving knife and fork, I ceremoniously entered the dining room.

Alison looked puzzled but at least she was still smiling.

"Stuffing?" I asked, scooping out the inside of the chicken. She smiled as I put the stuffing on her plate but her smile turned to laughter as the second scoop produced a plastic bag! Why would anybody put a plastic bag inside a chicken? Not to be defeated, I sliced off the tender leg of chicken, cutting through the white meat, then the pink meat and finally into the red meat in the joint. A small trickle of blood ran from the blade and started to form a pool on the dish.

"At least the potatoes are all right," I said in a final attempt to salvage something, but my errant fork simply refused to penetrate them.

"The wine's good," she said, smiling, but now I just sat at the table with my head on my hands.

Alison walked round the table and slipped her arms around my shoulders.

"It's the thought that counts. Besides, I didn't marry you for your cooking ability."

"I sometimes wonder why you married me at all."

Alison knelt down on the floor beside me, a serious look on her face. She took my hands in hers and gazed up into my eyes.

"Darling," she said. "I've got something very important to tell you. I know that you've been worried about work recently, and that things haven't been right at home, and so I feel that I've got to tell you this."

Here it was. She was going to tell me about an affair she had had. I could handle that. I just dreaded hearing that she was going to leave me.

"I'm afraid you're stuck with me forever. I love you now just as much as I did when I married you."

"Even if I'm out of work and all I can cook is beans?"

"Well, I usually shell Broad Beans first, but that's just me. You cook them whatever way you want to."

I cannot describe the feeling of joy and relief I felt as we held each other, laughing, crying and just being as one.

Did we eat that night? I cannot remember. We probably finished the wine.

As we lay in bed, I tried to explain my feelings to Alison. I mentioned the diary, and how it changed my perspective on life.

"Forget the diary," she said. "We haven't needed it so far."

But I could not forget something that made sense out of life. Something which has taught me the true value of life and what really mattered to me.

"If you can't forget it, write it down for other people to read. If it changed your life as much as you say, perhaps it could help others. I'm happy with my life. I'm happy with you and I'm not going to let some old diary come between us! Start writing it tomorrow."

She stroked my face with this last comment and we kissed. Whether we actually made love I cannot remember, but I have never felt such love as I did that night lying next to my wife, safe and contented.

I slept better that night than I had done in weeks. My life was back to normal, but somehow different. I felt like smiling. Perhaps that was why people, like the girl behind desk one, looked down on me. She had the same uncertainties in life that most people had, but she had a job. That put her one-step up the ladder. I no longer had any doubts about life. I knew where my true values lay and I did not need to invent anything to enhance my life. Of course, I still did not have a job, but that would come and I would not trade my newfound knowledge and security for any job.

Alison wished me luck before she took the children to school. It seemed a long time since she had done that, and somehow this told me that day would be lucky.

# CHAPTER 21

It took a couple of days for Alison's luck to filter through, but it finally happened one rainy day as I was giving the job centre window a final look before going home.  A short, balding man in a jacket and tie looked in the door and sighed at the length of the queue.

"I'm not waiting in that!" he said.

"If you really want a job you'll wait."

I smiled at this little man to show solidarity with a fellow job seeker.

"I'm not looking for work," he said sounding very irritated.

I gave him a puzzled look.

"Three weeks ago I instructed the job centre to put up an advert for a fork truck driver. I've been waiting desperately all this time only to find that they've got no record of my application!"

My ears pricked up at the prospect of work. I had driven fork trucks on sites.

"I'm looking for work as a fork truck driver," I said enthusiastically. "It would save you queuing…."

The man thought for a moment before his face stretched into a big smile.

"It could be a lucky day for both of us," he grinned. "The job is permanent you know. Is it a permanent job you're looking for?"

I went out of my way to convince him that I wanted the job. I went with him to a large warehouse and showed him what I could do on a truck. It was much easier driving on an even surface and the man was suitably impressed. He asked me if I could start the next day. I told him I would start yesterday if I could!

I could hardly contain my excitement as we shook hands and I left the warehouse. What to other people must seem like a mundane factory job was all I needed to complete my life. I could go to work in the morning, do my work and come home to live the important part of my life. I would be able to invent stories for the girls while I was at work, and look forward to telling them at night-time.

The look of achievement on my face when I got home told Alison the good news before I even opened my mouth, but she listened excitedly just the same.

"What rate are they starting you on?" she asked.

I had to confess that it had not occurred to me to ask. I was just so happy to be working again.

We both played with the girls until they were tired out. Then we spent a couple of hours talking before having an early night together. It seemed such a long time since we had done that.

# CHAPTER 22

The job was equally as good as I had hoped. I made more new friends there in the first few weeks than I made in years in other jobs. Perhaps it was because I was happy, contented with my life and understanding of other people. I no longer felt that people with different views on life from my own, were wrong. I did not seem to matter. I knew what I believed but as long as they were happy in their beliefs, where was the harm? Workmates eventually began to use me as a confidante, reasoning that I never let anything worry me and therefore must have my life together. Had I the inclination to do so, I could probably have converted many of them to my beliefs, but this would not change the world. The only influence I could have on the world was to try to change my little part of it for the better. I was no leader but people began to look to me for guidance. For every problem, I would encourage the person to consider the people who really mattered in his life, and make any decision by firstly considering them. Perhaps that is why they eventually gave me the dubious title of 'The Vicar'. Life was now so simple to me.

Alison noticed a change in me and suggested that she might also like to read the diary, but I did not think it was a good idea and she was easily dissuaded from the vague interest she showed. I loved her the way she was and I now liked myself in my newfound position of knowledge, so I saw no reason to alter the status quo.

I told her that I must finish reading the diary, but that it would not encroach on our quality time together. I read the rest of it during my lunch breaks at work or when the girls were in bed and Alison was watching one of her soaps.

I saw more of Nigel over the coming weeks and I even went to the hospital with Alison to visit his partner. I found myself giving advice and comfort to them both. The church community seemed to look down on gays, but I simply advised them to consider their love for each other in every decision they made and the rest of life would follow.

It amazed me that I was able to say this to people from a section of society I had previously looked down on. My amazement was nothing to Alison's utter astonishment.

"They're just two people who love each other," I found myself saying. "Everybody needs a bit of help and encouragement sometime in his life."

Alison's mouth was gaping open and I do not think it closed for some time.

My life was now complete. I was not out to change the world, simply to make my tiny part of it a little better. Global warming, whether natural or alien-induced would not have a dramatic effect on my life or that of my children. I knew where my values lay and the newfound respect from the people around me, including my family, was growing daily. I no longer looked down on people who were different from me, not even on the religious community. I found being pleasant to people very rewarding and being unpleasant very damaging, so I decided if I could not think of anything good to say to somebody, I would say nothing at all. I no longer had anything to prove.

I still wanted to finish reading the diary. I wanted to know how the priest used the information and what happened to the disk, so I would sit on my fork-truck eating my sandwiches as I poured over the rest of the story.

# CHAPTER 23

Fr. Ryan sat nervously in the bishop's office, as he waited for him to arrive. The bishop always kept him waiting and he was sure it was deliberate. The priest tried to banish these unchristian thoughts from his mind and instead focus on his explanation about the gun. It had all seemed so logical at the time, showing trust and respect to a section of society, to integrate them into the fold. Now, when he thought of explaining it to the bishop, it did seem rather foolish and far-fetched. Still, he did have the other matter to discuss and he had brought the disk with him as proof. The trick would be to overshadow one with the other.

The bishop gave a cursory glance in the priest's direction as he entered the room reading a document.

"Sit down," he barked.

The priest immediately obeyed.

The bishop took his place at his desk and continued to read his papers. He looked over his reading glasses and glared at Fr. Ryan.

The priest was squirming in his seat and jumped as the bishop slammed down the papers on the polished desk.

"Do you think I like being woken up in the early hours to find that one of my parish priests has been implicated in hiding weapons for street hoodlums!?"

"No, of course not," was the only reply he could think of although he knew it was feeble.

"What did you think you were doing?"

"I was trying to reach out to another section of God's people. Isn't that what I'm there for, to teach the word of God to as many people as I can? Isn't that why we're all here?

"Don't preach at me!" he snapped. "I'm your bishop! You're there to run the parish, not to get involved with street thugs! If you can't do that, I'll find someone who can!"

"I was going to hand in the gun. I wasn't hiding it for the gangs. I was trying to keep it off the streets."

"Then why didn't you hand it in? Why did you have to wait for the police to come round and arrest you?"

"I wasn't actually arrested. I was just helping the police..."

"Don't be pedantic with me," bellowed the bishop. "You were dragged to the police station late at night for having a gun in your possession. It was only because I managed to convince the chief constable that you were harmless, that got you off. He incidentally didn't appreciate being woken up either!"

Fr. Ryan had lost this battle and decided to bring up the other matter.

"Bishop," he said. "I realise that I have done a foolish thing and I can assure you that I will not repeat my mistake. I'm mortified by all the trouble I have caused you, but I now need to ask your help on another matter."

"What other matter? You've not been hiding drugs for them as well, have you?"

"No bishop. Even I'm not that foolish!"

The bishop sneered as Fr. Ryan desperately tried to find a way of explaining about the aliens.

"Do you agree that all nations should hear about Christ?"

"Patrick, if you want to be a missionary, you should have joined one of their orders!"

The bishop always used the priest's Christian name when he was really annoyed. It was like being verbally defrocked. But Fr. Ryan had to get him onside.

The man had said to him to tell only those he could trust and that he was in a unique position in which to do so. Whom could he trust if not his own bishop?

"What about aliens?"

The bishop's face was turning scarlet and the priest wished he could retract his last question.

"Have you lost your mind completely? I think you need a sabbatical, to help you to think things through more clearly. Do you realise what you've just said?"

"I know it sounds farfetched, but I have proof of alien life forms and we would be failing in our duty if we ignored God's creatures, even if they are from another planet."

"Proof? What proof?"

Fr. Ryan held out the disk and the bishop looked at it scornfully.

"What's this? Star trek? I'm going to arrange for another priest to take over your parish for a month or two so that you can have a long rest. You will announce this at Sunday mass. Say it's for your health, tell them anything you like, but be ready to go on Monday morning. I'll contact you with the details in the next couple of days. Now go, and try to keep out of trouble until Monday!"

"But I really don't think this is a good time for me to leave my parish. There's a lot of work I'm involved in."

"It wasn't a suggestion, Patrick!"

"Will you at least promise to look at the disk?"

"I'll look at your star trek disk, now go!"

Fr. Ryan left the room but did not breathe a sigh of relief until he got into his car, just in case the bishop called him back for another roasting. He drove home, content in the knowledge that he had set the ball rolling. He had completed his part in this mammoth venture.

He spent the evening relaxing, certain in the knowledge that it was all over. He was even looking forward to his holiday, wherever it might be.

The next day he visited the centre to let Mrs. Bryant know that he was going away for a couple of months. He said it was for health reasons and she was very concerned, but he put her mind at rest.

He felt good now that everything was settled and he started to clear out some old paperwork from the desk in the centre, and throw it in the big green bin out the back.

"I hear you're going away, father."

Spider's voice startled him, although he was happy to see the errant youth if only to say goodbye for a couple of months.

"Yes, that's right, but how did you find out?"

The next question took the priest by surprise.

"Your idea or theirs?"

The stilted conversation of the youth enabled him to ask many questions without revealing anything. This must be useful if he were arrested by the police, as he would be less likely to blurt out any information to which he was privy. It did make for difficult casual conversation. Fr. Ryan thought that it would be interesting to talk to Spider on a casual level when his guard was down. He was certainly an intelligent lad, just misguided. Of all the gang members, Spider was the one he knew best and he had a certain soft spot for the lad.

"They?"

"Why are you going away?"

He would have made a good police officer the way he asked questions without answering any, except of course for his criminal tendencies! Emotion was frowned upon by gang members, so he could not imagine Spider missing him. Why then did he seem concerned about him going away for a couple of months? Did he need another 'favour'?

"It's for health reasons," said the priest, feeling that he was being cross-examined.

"What's the matter with you? Are you ill?"

The questions were fired in rapid succession, hardly giving the priest time to consider his replies. This could only have been picked up from his past dealings with the police.

"No I'm not ill. I just need a holiday, somewhere I can relax away from the pressures of running the parish."

"Where are you going?"

Still the questions came.

"I'm not sure yet. It's being arranged as we speak. Look Spider, I'm just going on holiday. Don't you feel the need to take a holiday sometimes?"

The way the youth looked at him told the priest that the question was hypothetical. Gang leaders worked constantly, if only to defend their territories. Fr. Ryan wanted to reassure the youth that he was not abandoning him, especially now when he had started to gain his trust.

"If there's anything I can do for you before I go, you only have to ask.

Spider looked serious. This conversation was not normal, even by gangland standards. He seemed to want to convey something to the priest, but his street training forbade this.

"I mean it Spider, if there's anything I can do for you…."

"You've done me enough favours for me in the past, father, it's about time I did one for you."

This was a break for the priest. Spider wanting to do something for him. He dropped his head in thought, wondering what small favour he could ask, to begin the process of returning the youth to the fold. When he raised it again, he was alone.

# CHAPTER 24

Everything was now coming together for Fr. Ryan. He was no longer in trouble with the police, he had the gangs on his side and he had delivered the message to the bishop. Perhaps when he had looked at the disk, the bishop would cancel the priest's holiday, maybe even commend him for the risks he had taken in reaching out to all of God's children.

He sat there in quiet contemplation, hoping that the phone would ring and that the bishop would want to discuss the next step.

CRASH! The loud noise of the front door coming off its hinges hurled the priest from his chair. What now?

Suddenly the room was a hive of activity with police officers, some in plain clothes, milling about the house.

"Fr. Ryan?" said one of the plain-clothes officers. "You are under arrest under the moralities act. I have a warrant to search these premises for items of a pornographic nature."

The priest was in a daze and hardly heard the caution although he muttered an affirmation that he had understood it. He heard some noise from upstairs and frivolously wondered if his bedroom was tidy. A squat man with thin-rimmed glasses sat at the priest's computer, tapping the keys with obvious expertise.

Fr. Ryan slumped onto his chair as the sickening pictures reinstated themselves graphically on the screen. He could not look at them. He thought of the last words the bishop had said to him before he told him to get out. He had stayed out of trouble, or so he thought.

"Can you explain these pictures?"

The officious tone of the plain-clothes officer brought his mind back to the present. He wanted to tell him that the pictures were hacked into his computer without his knowledge.

"But I deleted them," was all he could think of saying.

"Then you admit it?"

A uniformed WPC entered the room with the diary in her hand.

"We found this," she said handing the book to the priest's inquisitor.

Fr. Ryan panicked and made an unsuccessful grab for the book. This contained details of the gun and other incriminating evidence. If they read it, the gangs would think he had betrayed them! Everything was happening around him, but his mind refused to accept it. He was standing outside his body, watching this dreadful thing happening to somebody else. He could not even pray for a way out, nothing was real!

His head was swimming and he imagined two uniformed officers stumbling into the room. Perhaps it was not his imagination. The hooded figure holding the sawn-off double-barrelled shotgun was certainly real, as was the hooded figure beside him

Fr. Ryan snatched the diary from the detective as the second dark figure pulled him to his feet and bundled him out of the room and over the front door that lay flat in the hallway. Powerful arms bundled him into a waiting car, which sped away into the night.

# CHAPTER 25

Fr. Ryan had only vague recollections of the journey or of his destination. When he finally came back to the world of reality, he found himself lying on a bed in a large room with high ceilings. A rather pretty young lady with long blond hair, jeans and a tasteless t-shirt, which just about covered her upper body, sat on a chair beside him mopping his brow with a wet flannel.

What would have been a pleasant awakening for most men was both shocking and compromising for a catholic priest.

He sat up far too suddenly, which made his head spin.

"He's awake," sang the sweet voice of this young temptress.

The door opened and Spider walked in. The priest was happy to see a familiar face, even though he had no idea of the situation he was in.

"Nice to have you back with us, father."

The youth seemed friendly enough but reading the facial expression of a gang member could be risky. He had to appraise the situation and the only way he could think of doing so was to ask the youth directly.

"Am I in trouble?" he ventured, dreading the answer.

"You're safe for now," was the stilted reply. "Have you met my girlfriend, Mandy? She'll look after you."

All thoughts of being in a compromising situation soon left the priest along with any suppressed feelings he might have had. This was Spider's girl, and nobody would dare hint at anything else!

The more the priest described the old Victorian house he was in, the more I recognised it. It gave me a certain affinity with him to know that I had stood in this place. I thought of other sites I had worked on and wondered about their history.

The diary was coming to an end and I felt that it had helped me to make sense of my life. At this point, I hoped it would do the same for the priest. I finished reading it one Saturday afternoon when Alison had taken the girls to her friend's house.

# CHAPTER 26

Fr. Ryan did not see Spider for the rest of the day. He had an en-suite bathroom he could use and he kept to his part of the house, despite hearing lots of activity from other rooms. He once suggested to Mandy, his constant companion, that it would be good if he could speak to Spider, to smooth things out.

"Best not disturb him when he's got business to take care of," she said pleasantly.

The look of dismay on the priest's face was apparent and Mandy added:

"Don't worry father, you'll be all right. He likes you."

This last comment made the priest feel more at ease. Mandy either could not or would not give him any information on his current situation, and after a while, he stopped asking.

That evening, as they sat there eating a takeaway pizza together, he thought of the absurdity of the situation he was in. He was a parish priest, wanted by the police, protected by the gangs and probably about to be defrocked by the bishop. Yet here he was in this calm place eating pizza with a pretty girl barely eighteen years old. He wondered what kind of an upbringing she must have had to be mixed up in all of this, what sins she would have to confess. The worst sin Fr. Ryan could ever remember committing as a child was when he used to drip washing-up liquid into his parent's fishpond, simply to watch the water boatmen struggling for their lives, something about which he felt a strange remorse even to this day. Yet here was this kind soul giving comfort to a priest in distress.

She flicked back her long hair with her hand and then gave the priest's hand a squeeze.

"I'll let you get to bed now father. You must be tired and Spider wants to talk to you tomorrow. Don't worry," she said as she smiled and left the room.

It seems that the house was in a bad state of repair even at that time. There were gaping cracks down some of the walls and the ceiling was not even attached in places. It looked like some renovation work had been started, but this just left holes in walls and made the structure look even more unsafe. The room was sparsely furnished with an old once-green three-piece suite, a bed and a dilapidated wooden table in the corner attempting to pose as an antique. Nevertheless, it was safe and nobody would be looking for him here.

Fr. Ryan had only just woken when Spider came into the room carrying two mugs of steaming tea.

"Morning father," he said pleasantly. "Sorry about the kidnap, it was the only way we could get you out of there."

The priest was in a quandary. Spider had taken a serious risk in dragging him out of the grasp of the police, but still Fr. Ryan could not condone his actions. He was a catholic priest, not a criminal. He had done nothing wrong.

"Spider what's going on? I'm not a criminal and I shouldn't be running from the police."

"What did they arrest you for? Was it pornography?"

"Yes, but it was all a big mistake. How did you know anyway?"

"Just an educated guess. It's what they usually use for the clergy. It's the one thing that everybody will believe."

"Dc you believe I'd do such a thing?"

"Nc, but it doesn't matter what I think. All those times you helped me out with the police, did it ever occur to you that I might be innocent?"

Fr. Ryan bowed his head in shame. He had often spoken up for Spider oy making excuses for his behaviour, while accepting the police charges against him.

"Don't worry father. Most of the time you were right to think like that."

The stilted conversation of the street had disappeared and a cold logic had taken its place. The priest had wanted a normal conversation with the youth but now that he had his wish, he was fumbling around for something to say.

"People see gangs on the street and lump us all together. Do you see any needle tracks on my arms?"

He pulled up his sleeves and held out his tattooed arms for the priest to inspect.

"You won't find them on any of my friends either. The most I do is smoke a little weed to relax."

"But you fight….."

"Of course we fight, but not for power. We fight for security, we run a serious business and sometimes things get a little out of hand."

"But you can't blame people for thinking you're like all the rest."

"Blame them? You don't understand father, that's what they're supposed to think. That's our cover. Everyone sees us as drug-ridden low-life and they keep away from us. OK, I'm not saying that we don't break the occasional law, well, quite a lot of laws I suppose but we don't go around killing everybody who gets in our way, like some governments do. Take your situation. You're a catholic priest arrested on pornography charges."

"I'm innocent of those charges."

"OK, let's say I believe you. How are you going to prove it?

"Well certainly not by running away. Somebody put that on my computer without my knowledge. Surely a computer expert could prove that?"

"If he wanted to, but suppose it came out in court that the data was downloaded from your computer. Perhaps somebody broke in and downloaded it."

"I think I'd have noticed a break-in."

"Have you let anybody else use your computer?"

"No, nobody"

"It must have been the police then."

"The police? I can't believe the police would do it!"

The youth gave a big sigh, a bit like the man in the confessional only Spider was smiling.

"The ones who arrested you weren't your regular copper on the beat. They're all right, nice blokes some of them. These ones were much higher up the ladder."

There was a pause before the youth continued.

"I'm sorry father but you don't know a lot about the world."

"What do you mean?"

"They wanted you out of the way so they arrested you on some minor charge so that they could gain access to your computer. Then they could take you out of the system any time they wanted to by planting something on your hard drive."

"I don't believe the police would do that. Besides, if it happened when I was with the police, it couldn't have been me."

"Did you see anybody else at the station?"

"Just the duty officer, but there must be records."

"I'll bet you won't find any!"

"Anyway, why would they go to all this trouble to get me out of the way? I'm no threat to them!"

"Now you're into my business, information, the most powerful commodity in the world. You have access to information that you shouldn't have access to. That makes you dangerous."

"What information? I don't know what you're talking about.

"Perhaps the disk you downloaded?"

"Yes but nobody knows about that apart from you lot, oh and the bishop of course."

Spider leapt to his feet.

"You told the bishop!

"Yes, I gave him a copy, but I didn't say where the information came from."

"Wait here," he said as he rushed out of the room.

A light-hearted thought crossed the priest's mind. Perhaps Spider was frightened of the bishop too! He looked up as Mandy entered the room and tried to find some comfort in her face but she just frowned and raised her eyebrows.

It was three hours before he saw Spider again. The priest did not know if he was a prisoner, but felt sure he would not be able to get out of the house. Anyway, where would he go? If Spider was right, and the priest could not think of any reason he would lie, then he would be in trouble wherever he went. He thought of the disk under the ciborium and decided that he must tell somebody where it was, just in case something happened to him and the bishop forgot

237

to read his copy.  He would turn to the only person he could trust, he would tell Spider.

Mandy left the room as Spider entered.  She seemed to know what business concerned her and what she was not supposed to hear.

"Right father.  Word on the street is that you've got a lot of people looking for you.  We'll have to move you round a bit, but you'll be safe here for a couple of days."

"Spider," said the priest gravely.  "I have to tell you something very important.  It's something you might not believe but I think it's the cause of all this trouble.  Do you remember that disk I downloaded?"

"What, the one about the captured alien and the Earth being condemned?"

Father Ryan was totally astounded.

"How could you possibly know about that?"

"It was the reason we rescued you.  You surely don't think that we'd carry guns and charge-down the police for some priest who downloads porn onto his computer? Perhaps I should explain. We deal in information."

"What kind of information? I mean, how do you deal in it?"

"Sometimes we're hired to steal information for industrial espionage, but usually it's just for blackmail."

The matter-of-fact way that Spider gave this information to him shocked even one who was used to hearing confessions. Was he showing trust or did he know that the priest was far too frightened ever to have said anything?

"Spider, that's terrible!"

Spider laughed.

"Don't worry father, they can all afford it. Take the recent case of a high court judge who liked to visit massage parlours. He could have been blackmailed into throwing the trial of some low-life dealer. We got in there first and blackmailed him for money. He paid for his crime and won't repeat it. He then returned to being a model citizen. It cut out the expense of a trial and didn't cause any pain to the man's family. He was the one who got himself into the situation and he was the only one who paid. It's a public service."

Fr. Ryan was not in the least convinced by the youth's explanation, but now was not the time to admonish him over it

"How did you get hold of the disk? I was the only one in the room."

"Yes, you and a lot of electronic equipment, but don't worry. All information is vetted and if it had been porn you were downloading, we'd have simply wiped it."

"Or blackmailed me with it!"

"We wouldn't have blackmailed you father."

He paused just long enough for the priest to feel guilty about making his last statement, then he smiled.

"You don't have anything we want!"

He hoped the youth was joking.

"What did you think of the disk, and have you read all of it?"

"It fits in with other information we've got. Just never had it on official government documents before. The question is how did you get hold of government passwords? You're a priest. I thought you just went round blessing people."

"I can't tell you where the information came from, but if it proves that there's an alien world out there, the church needs to get involved so that we can teach them about Jesus."

"Well no one else has access to our website and it wasn't any of us who turned you in. That just leaves the church."

Although he did not like the bishop, he would defend him to the hilt on corruption charges.

"The bishop would never have turned me in."

"He wouldn't have to. All he would have to do is send the disk further up the chain of command. There's always corruption in any organisation and they will fight to make sure it does not become public."

"But the man who gave me this information wanted me to convince the church to act. Why would he do that if it's full of corruption?"

"Beats me," shrugged the youth.

"Have you ever heard of Opus Dei?"

"I've heard of them," said Spider. "They're a pretty nasty group of right-wing militants who seem to like to go round whipping each other."

"Then they do exist," the priest affirmed.

"They exist all right but they're way out of my league! That's a group that really has some clout! Don't get mixed up with them father. They make the Marquis De Sade seem like a tame eccentric."

"What about MIR?"

"Never heard of them, but there must be some group coordinating all this mayhem. Father, I'm sorry you had to find out about the church in this way."

Spider seemed genuinely sorry for the priest. Perhaps he really did like him. It was now time for Fr. Ryan to put the youth's mind at rest.

"Spider, I'm not naïve enough to think that the church is perfect. We've all heard about the Borgias and Pope Joan. Just because the church gets run badly from time to time, doesn't make its main teaching bad. God will watch over us and if a person truly believes, that person will be saved."

"I'm very happy to hear you say that father. We'll talk again but now I've got some business to take care of."

As Spider stood up to leave, his last comment now made more sense to the priest. He thought the answer to his single-sentence sermon, however, to be a little patronising, but it was a start.

"What will you do with the disk?" he asked as Spider opened the door to leave.

"I'll send a copy to some friends and they'll distribute it as they see fit."

"I hope you can trust them!"

"That's the one thing I am sure of!"

# CHAPTER 27

It was ten pm when the door opened and the huge figure of Donkey thundered through carrying a brown paper bag in his podgy hands.

"Hope you like Chinese," he said with what could almost have been interpreted as a cheerful grin.

Fr. Ryan looked at him in astonishment and it was a good few seconds before he could say anything.

"I thought you and Spider were enemies!"

One edge of the youth's mouth curled up briefly once again.

"Naw."

"But you fight!"

"Just a bit of friendly rivalry from time to time, but he's a good man. I'd trust him with my life!"

He put down the bag, which Mandy eagerly opened.

"We'll have to move you soon father. Things are hotting up a bit out there."

Donkey left the room and Mandy and the priest tucked in to their meal.

Mandy would leave the priest alone to say his office, during which time he also filled in the diary. He seemed to be trying to make sense of the whole thing. He missed not being able to say mass and realised he could not stay in hiding forever. He aired these views to Spider when he came to bring him the local paper, but the youth told him it was too dangerous to show himself yet.

The priest was shocked when he read in the paper that he had been ill and had gone away to recuperate. The columnist also expressed his best wishes for a speedy recovery. They had already got him out of the way, at least on paper. There was no mention of his being kidnapped or of the fact that they had come to arrest him. So what would happen if he were to walk into a police station and hand himself in? Could they still make the charges stick? The same thing would apply if they found him. Yet they were still looking for him and they could claim that the press had been misinformed or that it was a clever trick to bring him into the open.

He put the diary in a wall cavity, which had been opened up by subsidence, and prayed for guidance.

It was late evening when Spider walked into the room, a serious look on his face. Fr. Ryan was about to speak to him when Donkey rushed in.

"Mandy's been arrested," he said, reverting to the stilted conversation used for 'business' matters.

"Good," replied Spider. "It'll keep her out of the way when the trouble starts."

This comment shocked the priest. Spider's girlfriend had just been arrested and all he could say was good?

"Why was she arrested?" he asked.

"Probably to find out where we're keeping you. I knew it wouldn't take them long to work out that we were behind the kidnap. Don't worry, she won't talk. My information tells me they've hired a Rat gang to look into it. They mean business!"

"Rat gang?"

"Hired thugs, usually mercenaries dressed to look like a street gang. It makes it look like a turf war which everybody accepts."

"Hired by whom?"

Spider shrugged.

"Special branch or one of the other government organisations. Don't worry, we've got friends to help us take care of them. It's not the first time this has happened. We'll move you sometime tomorrow evening before the trouble starts."

The youth turned to Donkey.

"Get that disk to Birmingham," he ordered.

It seemed strange to see the two youths, whom the priest had thought were bitter enemies, working together.

"Let me send someone else. You'll need me when the trouble starts."

Spider thought for a moment.

"Come on Spider, how far would you get without me to look after you?"

Spider smiled as he nodded his assent.

"You'd probably never find Birmingham anyway."

The youths went to leave the room but Fr. Ryan called to Spider.

"Can I talk to you for a minute," he asked him.

Spider walked back and sat on the chair near the priest.

"What's on your mind father?"

"There's going to be blood spilt, isn't there?"

"Don't worry about it. Our back up's already in place. They think they're only dealing with a dozen or so. They won't be prepared for what we've got planned."

"You've done so much for me, but I don't want any blood to be spilt on my behalf."

"No way of avoiding it now father. The Rat gang's already in London."

"But why do they want me so badly. They've seen the disk and as you say, they can control me anyway."

"It's not the disk they want, it's the man who gave you the information. The longer they wait the more time he has to disappear."

"But I don't know who the man is. I've never actually seen him."

"That may be, but do you think you can convince them of that? It's better you stay hidden for as long as possible."

"Why are you risking all this for me?"

"The more you let the government grind you down, the less alive you are. Besides, I told you we traded information and this will be some trade!"

Spider once again stood up to go.

"I'll leave Tony with you tomorrow. He's young but you can trust him, and I don't want him caught-up in the trouble. Somebody will bring you some food later but I'm going to have to leave you on your own most of the time. We need to plan for tomorrow night."

Fr. Ryan stood up and extended his hand towards the youth.

"Thanks for everything you've done," he said.

Spider looked a little embarrassed as they shook hands.

"No problem father. I know you'd have done the same for me."

With that, Spider left the room leaving Fr. Ryan alone, in every conceivable way.

By this time, I believe that the priest had decided he could not continue to live this way. His Christian upbringing would not allow him to be the cause of violence, whatever justification there appeared to be. He prayed that night harder than he had ever prayed before. He knew that God was on his side but he feared the injustices of man. There did not seem any logic to the course that events had taken in his life. Had God himself been standing in front of him it would have been easy to explain the decisions he had made. God knew what was in his heart, but it was man with all his failings who would accuse him.

He prayed harder, trying not to lose his faith now, when he needed it most. The effects of being convicted of a crime were more far-reaching than the effects on his life. The church would suffer with yet another priest being convicted on pornography charges. The people of his parish would suffer and wonder how much of his teaching was hypocritical. His family would suffer pain and humiliation.

He tried to imagine standing in a court, explaining that it was all a mistake, and the people in the public gallery nudging each other and claiming that they knew there was something odd about this priest. It is stunning how quickly people turn against a person, however well they previously thought of him. In fact, the better they thought of him, the quicker they seem to turn. It seems to be accepted that children from 'broken marriages' are more likely to commit crime than children from stable homes, yet they are given excuses, they are understood. Such charity would never be extended to any leader accused of a crime. People not only readily believe the accusations, but even add little bits onto them in the assumption that they are probably true.

He imagined the jury returning a verdict of guilty and the gavel falling to end his life. What would prison be like? Would he be allowed to say mass? Could he bear the derision of the other inmates?

He had prayed for an inroad into gangland life, but to teach them, not to be a part of that life. But perhaps being part of their lives was the only position from which to teach them. Was this what God had in mind for him, to live the life of an outlaw and preach from within that society?

I have always believed that many religious people justify taking the easiest route through any difficult decision, by saying that it is what God wanted them to do.

'If God had wanted me to stay with my partner, he wouldn't have let me love this other person.'

It worked for the crusaders:

'With God on our side we're free to rape, pillage and murder these heathens.'

It works for any wartime situation:

'We're fighting with God on our side so we're bound to win.'

It works for the people who make these decisions:

'We're fighting for God and country.'

Leading an outwardly religious life seems to justify many decisions. I cannot think of any English monarch, prime minister or American president who was an atheist. Even evidence given in court is treated with suspicion if the promise to tell the truth is not made to a God; such is the power of religion.

Fr. Ryan was a different breed, that rare breed which makes decisions on deep held beliefs, rather than convenient interpretations of those beliefs. He took his lead from the life of Christ and how he faced his accusers, despite offers to fight on his behalf from Peter and the rest. In fact, he told them to put down their swords, not to fight on his behalf.

Whether it was his faith in God or the pure bravery of a man who was convinced that he was taking the right path, I will never know, but I have a profound respect for this man's decision. He could have decided on the easy route, to let others fight for him, and he would have been justified in most people's eyes in believing that it was God who had placed him in this unique position.

His last entry in the diary read as follows:

I am innocent of all the crimes of which I am accused. I have a total respect and undying gratitude for the faith and trust shown by those who have tried to help me. With God's help, I will never betray that trust. I will make my escape tomorrow when there is only one person here, and lay myself in the hands of the authorities, and on the mercy of God.

# CHAPTER 28

It was like reading a novel and finding the last page missing. I had to know what happened to him. Every time a clergyman is convicted of this sort of crime, people tend to say 'oh another one', but I am sure there really cannot be that many. I spent hours at the library, trying to find some reference to a catholic priest being brought to court, but to no avail. I thought that perhaps he had got off; I certainly hoped so!

I began to visit bars in the area of the church when Alison was visiting her friends. It had not happened many years before so I thought someone might remember it.

I met two elderly gentlemen, a little worse for wear who had differing opinions on the fate of the priest. They were of Irish descent with the proverbial talent for telling a story. After I had bought them a couple of drinks, their memories seemed to return.

"Would that be Fr. Pat Ryan? I knew him well," said Sean, the lesser inebriated of the two. "You'll never find a better priest, died suddenly while he was on holiday. Heart attack I think it was."

His drinking partner, whose name I never did catch although he told me twice, had a different recollection of events.

"It was some gang that had him killed," he whispered. "He got mixed up in some drug deal, all very hush hush."

Having difficulty wading through the drunken Irish brogue, I made my excuses and left them arguing about who had the right version. Hoping to catch them sober in the future I asked if they would be there on the following Sunday and at what time.

"Straight after mass has finished," they said, almost in unison.

Weeks of work and hours of talking to people had resulted in two drunks who could not even agree on their story. Still, at least they had heard of the priest and I was determined to catch them sober the following week.

I did not visit the church where Fr. Ryan had been. I am not certain if I would have received a frank answer. I preferred to hear it from someone who had no connection with the case.

I told Alison about my detective work and she was happy.

"I feel a bit guilty about going to see my friends without you," she said, "but I know you wouldn't enjoy an afternoon of girlie talk."

"I don't mind," I said. "It gives me some peace and quiet for a change!"

Alison hit me, but only in fun.

The following Sunday I ran Alison and the girls to church and headed straight for the bar. I wanted to be there before mass had finished. Alison said she would get a lift home so there was no need for me to pick her up.

# CHAPTER 29

The bar was empty when I arrived but I was only halfway through my first pint when the place began to fill up. As Sean and his friend approached the bar, their drinks were ready for them.

"Remember me from last week?" I asked as I walked up to where they were seated. "I wondered if you've remembered any more about Fr. Ryan."

"Who?"

"Fr. Ryan. You remember. The priest who died suddenly? Fr. Pat Ryan?"

The two shook their heads in bewilderment.

"But you told me about him last week. You said you knew him!"

"Ah, well you know when you've had a wee bit too much to drink you sometimes remember things that were never there for you to know in the first place."

The logic was stunning. Then I thought of how I got them talking the week before.

"I'll just go for a leak, then I'll get the drinks in."

While I was in the toilet, I wondered how many drinks they would manage to con out of me before they remembered the priest. By the time I re-entered the bar, the men had gone.

That was it, now I would have to visit the church!

It was only a brisk ten-minute walk, enough time for me to think about what I would say to the priest.

I did not see the man who trapped me in a headlock. I did not see his accomplice in the alley I was dragged into. The only thing I saw was the wall as I was slammed into it, arms pinned behind my back. One of the men grabbed my hair and held my head facing the wall.

"My wallet's in my back pocket," I gasped, still a little winded from the heavy contact. "Take the money, there's not much there. There's no need for violence."

I felt my wallet slip out of my pocket and was relieved that my ordeal would soon be over. There were footsteps in the alley and I felt a powerful grip on the back of my neck.

"Nice looking family," said the voice from behind.

I remembered the photo I kept in my wallet of Alison and the girls. I felt that the man was threatening them and I struggled with every ounce of strength in my body, but I could not move.

"You've been asking a lot of questions. Why do you want to know about Fr. Ryan?"

"Who?"

The grip tightened on my neck.

"All right!" I screamed. Just let go of my neck! I found his diary in an old house I was working on around here. I just wanted to know what happened to him."

"Why?"

"He seemed a decent man and I thought I'd write about a book about the last few months of his life."

"What was in this diary?"

His grip eased on my neck as I relayed the contents of the diary. He asked a couple of short questions but mainly listened with apparent interest. I ended by telling him that somebody had told me the priest had been murdered because of a drug deal, but that I did not believe that after having read the diary.

"This book," he said. "Don't you think it might get a lot of people into trouble?"

"It was just an idea," I said, not wanting any more trouble than I already had. "I don't have to write it!"

There was a pause as the man thought about what I had said.

"Fr. Ryan was one of the bravest men I had ever known. People should hear about him. You go ahead and write your book. Just forget about any names or places you've read about."

Even though my arms were still being held in a painful position, I had to know what I came here to find out.

"What happened to him in the end?"

"The lad who was with him left him alone to say some prayers that he had to say every day. He slipped out the door when the lad wasn't watching. The Rat gang must have come across him by chance in the street. They took him to a building site near here, stripped him naked and beat the crap out of him. They knocked bits of broken bottle into his head to try to make him talk. He never told them where he'd been staying, where the disk was or who gave him the information, not even when they nailed him to the side of the site hut! He was dead by the time the gangs found him."

"He died by crucifixion?"

I was beginning to feel ill. I could not believe this kind of thing could happen in London.

"No. Somebody took pity on him. He was found with a knife sticking out of his chest. He was stabbed through the heart. At least that part was quick."

Now I really felt like I wanted to be sick but I was still pinned against the wall.

"You've got your ending now; make sure you write it as it happened. Someone will come and collect the diary soon, so make sure you've got all the information you need from it."

As my wallet was slipped back into my pocket, I realised that it contained my address. Even with the sickness I felt n my stomach and the pain in my arms, I knew this was a one-off opportunity and I had to ask one last question.

"The disk," I said. "What happened to the disk?"

I felt the man's forearm rest on my shoulder and noticed the spider-web tattoo on his elbow. His lips were so close to my ear that I felt his breath.

"The disk is all right where it is," he whispered, "and you won't be visiting this area again."

"No," was my timid reply as the grips on me were released and I leant my arms against the wall and vomited.

# CHAPTER 30

A well-dressed man knocked on my door a couple of weeks later saying he had a book to collect. I calmly handed it over, after which he thanked me politely and left.

That was the last contact I had with the diary or with anybody connected with it. I changed the names and places as I promised and now I would have difficulty in remembering the original ones, even if I thought it was wise.

My life had been changed by reading the diary of a man who lived his life according to a God in whom I no longer believed. The woman in the park had made me see that it does not matter what you believe as long as it is based on love. Yet I consider my outlook on life is now more in tune to what I formerly believed Christianity was all about.

I do not know which parts of the governmental conspiracy theories are true, and I do not really care. I believe that the chances of my finding out are very remote. My life is now built around my family and the little corner of the world that I touch. I am not big enough to be troubled by MIR and I never want to be. I do not ask my friends about their politics or by what name they call God. I only hope that by goodwill and friendship, we can all end our lives with happy thoughts and enter our respective heavens.

Alison has never read the diary, she says that she is happy with her beliefs and does not want to change them. She still takes the girls to church and I still drive her there, before spending an hour in the park to feed the birds. I often think of the old lady even now, but her words of wisdom were really brought home to me even before I had finished reading the diary. Alison came into the living room looking very upset.

"Have you read this?" she asked, holding up the local paper. "It says that an old lady was found dead in a park. She had no family. It's so sad to hear that somebody can die alone without anyone caring."

Tears began to well up in her eyes and I held her tightly.

"Perhaps she wasn't alone in her mind," I said.

How could I tell her that I was the one who left her there? I was not sad for the old lady because I knew a little about her life and I knew that she did not die alone. I was sad because Alison was sad. We were one.

There was still one burning question on my mind, something I had to ask my wife but could not find the right time or words to ask it. The question seemed unfair and yet I still felt compelled to ask it, if only to follow one of the last pieces of advice that the old lady had given. It seemed very odd that a big tough man like me was afraid to ask his wife a simple question, but such is the nature of man's insecurity.

The question just popped out one day without any timing or forethought. It happened just after we put the girls to bed.

"Alison," I said, not quite believing what I was about to ask her. "Can I ask you a question?"

She smiled, looked into my eyes and rested her hands on my waist.

"Do you love God more than you love me?"

Her arms left my waist and slid around my neck, drawing our bodies close.

"Darling," she whispered. "There's a little part of God in all of us and we show our love for him by loving each other. You must have more of God in you because I love you more than anyone else."

She was right. I now had a little bit of God in me, even though I did not know by what name to call her. But now I know for certain that the name does not matter.

# EPILOGUE

The other evening, a man with a Bible in his hand, came into my local pub trying to convert people to some religion or other. I asked him why he believed in the Bible. He told me that it was because it was the word of God.

He then asked me what I thought that the individual could do to help stop all the violence in the world.

"I can only speak for myself," I replied. "Personally I think that Adolph Hitler always kept his boots nice and shiny."

I left the bemused man standing there as I exited the bar.

# ABOUT THE AUTHOR

Des Birch was born in Limerick, Eire but moved to England when he was a baby. He moved from Buckinghamshire to Norfolk when he was ten, but attended a private school near Southampton. He has two children whom he has raised on his own since they were ten and eight respectively. He works in engineering but has gained a BSc and a Dip. Pol. Con. with the Open University. He also gained a TEFL diploma with which he spent two years teaching in Spain. Des now lives in Norwich with his wife Julie.

www.ingramcontent.com/pod-product-compliance
Lightning Source LLC
Chambersburg PA
CBHW061558170626
46811CB00001B/248